# SLE

## A Utopian Bestiary

*Michele Spina*

translated
by
Ann Colcord
with
Hugh Shankland

First published in Great Britain in 2001 by Colin Smythe Limited,
Gerrards Cross, Buckinghamshire SL9 8XA

**British Library Cataloguing-in-Publication Data**
A catalogue record for this book is available
from the British Library
**ISBN 0-86140-437-8**



First published in North America in 2001 by Dufour Editions
P.O.Box 7, Chester Springs, PA 19425-0007
**ISBN 0-8023-1334-5**

Produced in Great Britain
Typeset by Art Photoset Ltd., Beaconsfield, Buckinghamshire
Printed and bound by
The Guernsey Press Co.Ltd., P.O.Box 57, Vale, Guernsey

# SLEEP

for Margaret
with much love
from Ann

BY THE SAME AUTHOR

*West of the Moon* (1994)
*Night and Other Short Stories (1998)*

# CONTENTS

Big-bellies, worms, whores, toads, lantern jaws wander through a provincial maze that is not quite city and not quite country in an unnamed land that is a cradle of the rights of the strongest. It is pointless to try to identify this land (some clues might lead one to suspect that it is Brobdingnag or the Land of the Houyhnhnms). What does matter is that this is the setting for an unresolved moral conflict between the internal forum and the external forum: a tale of the anguished unfolding of the inner zone of moral decisions in the face of the decline of values, conduct and taste, and, ultimately, of that fabric of conventions which forms the basis for judgements made by the external forum. The individual conscience becomes at the same time both judge and culprit, victim and executioner. This is nothing new since Baudelaire, but here the attraction of a limitless and perilous inner freedom has become weariness and dejection at the prospect of a freedom which has all the futile insubstantiality of Kierkegard's 'infinite evil of the possible' and does not even imply an effort of will or an exploration.

# SLEEP

The bare walls, the mild temperature, the silence and within the silence the distant hum of the office machines, the light and the day slowly slipping towards sunset, all his surroundings, ceaselessly considered and reconsidered, appeared to provide the ideal conditions for sleep. But aside from the fact that he suffered from incurable insomnia, an office is no place for a sleep, no matter how modern. To distract himself, he crossed to the window and stood there looking out onto an internal courtyard, so empty and still that as the hours of the day went by abandon and solitude seemed to mount its walls like liquid shadow, although in reality not a shadow stirred beneath the unvarying glow of the sky. There was wind in the sky and the sun shone brilliantly somewhere; not above the courtyard but over some other district of the city or even some other place faraway, eccentric and probably tropical.

The courtyard, small but ostentatiously elegant, was paved in the same pale grey stone as its walls. Each wall of the two lower stories had four windows set within ornate semi-columns crowned by arches, while those of the third and uppermost storey above the arches had only three square windows surrounded by plain mouldings. The effect was completed by a heavy cornice which like a frame around a picture now contained the blue of the windswept sky, looking so detached from all worldly concerns as to suggest a profound vocation for sleep.

The more he thought about it, every single thing, every instant, appeared to present an invitation to sleep. The physical presence of the window, the sky beyond the window, the calm light not only in the office but surrounding objects he didn't see (but whose names arose in his mind moment by moment with the simplicity of picture-book images: rose, vase, gull, tree, or others that kept arriving along the thread of interminable associations) seemed to him to have the immediacy of sleep.

The present, he said to himself, anything present or just the simple presence of the present is a prelude to sleep: from the here and now one slips so easily into a sound sleep ... or rather one should. Not in his case. What hindered him from crossing the threshold between the present and sleep was, he believed, a certain befuddlement of his thought-process: a confusion and mental tangle in which not only the threads of logic got lost but even those of the imagination. Just as he was dropping off he would suddenly find himself right up against a skein of the unthinkable. *Quid tum*? he would wonder and wake with a jump. But up to that moment everything would seem to be going so well: he proceeded as it were by salient points, swaying like a reed in the wind from one picture to another, now towards a gloomy dinner with many places set for guests, next towards a winter solstice luminous and somewhat chilly, as though the blankets had slipped from the bed. What all these introductions to sleep had in common was the raw presence of the present or, to avoid tautology, better to say the presence of life as an inevitable but presumably happy necessity, no matter in what direction his destiny might lurch. But I've said this or something very like it many times before. What else can I say? he wondered.

I repeat myself, he grumbled. And yet, he added, hoping to console himself, there is always some slight variation when one says the same thing. *Non nova sed noviter.* On the other hand it was precisely the appearance of these variations that disconcerted him; they presented themselves first as innocuous amendments, and the moment they were accepted they turned into eccentric mistakes and irremediable travesties. Maybe it's the office, he told himself, the tedium of spending so much time sitting down.

He shook off his torpor by thinking of the wind which had been strong since this morning, the wind over the sea which must be whipped to a storm by now, unleashing towering waves against the high railway embankment behind which huddled low warehouses and little workshops and miserable flimsy houses whose pale walls seemed to be stubbornly waiting for some benign event to relieve the general gloom of the situation, perhaps even releasing that special elation and high spirits that are reputedly the peculiar attribute of the poor. There were mostly brothels in that street and one in particular he could have described from memory, accurate in every detail. More than just good memory, he felt this descriptive accuracy came from a minute accumulation of forlorn affections, of passions as chill as childhood winters: something damp and windblown, something as solitary and fleeting as an ailing dog; a sight as desolate as Sunday viewed from a brothel door. Perhaps it was not so much a case of an actual doorway, more a mental contrast and comparison between the rainy light in the street and the lukewarm light in the brothel where the pinks, without ever being in great abundance, seemed to him the best of all things he had ever been vouchsafed to see. In any case, the brothel was not truly welcoming, for also inside there and even while the storm was raging they found ways of saying disagreeable things: for example, that his chin hid not only his neck but also his handsome new tie.

In the light of the interior two young whores wearing low-cut pink dresses revealing the livid skin over their ribs were chattering idly, at times intertwining their arms in various ways. Even when straining his ears to catch what the two were saying he could still at moments hear the pounding of the sea beyond the railway yard. That pounding even merged with the conversation punctuating statements such as 'she's tired'; and words like 'bum' 'lawyer' 'coat' which floated idly while the palest and loneliest of the women wandered from one group to another looking lost. Always, at the end of these or similar intimacies, the sudden booming of the sea brutally injected the presence of time: the physical reality of the instant, but now alert and all-seeing: the grey face of destiny with no concessions to pink, although, thinking back on it with the memories filtering through the lashes of pressing sleep, at least some touch of pink had always appeared somewhere, on the knobby tops of skinny buttocks, for instance.

In any case now, no matter how hard he thought about sleep he still wasn't sleeping; and so the only present whose presence, or burden, he could feel was an ever-waking present, extended to everyone everywhere on earth. At the centre of this immense space, even his office, protective and modern and restful as it might look to him, was no more than one aspect of the vacuous objective vastness, the face of an alien universe staring back at him: effigy of shipwreck and oblivion, not rest. Because, the more he thought about it, what else could be expected of this deserted emptiness, this boundless Libya of time, if not the levelling of the day? What was there to expect from this day now or other days as stagnant as this, in which the mild temperature, the silence or hum of the office machines, the light and the slow slipping of that light towards sunset could contain no other variant but the hope of sleep?

'No, no!' he said aloud, waving his hand about as though to fend off evil. 'Let's try to get some sleep instead!' After all, what can be more simple than sleeping? Try! Take an example at random: some character, anyone at all, weary from his labours let's say, or dazed by too much wine and also exhausted by the heat (in this instance it's summertime, when sleep comes more easily) staggers over to a huge bed and flops out on it, weight on his left arm, cheek pressing into the pillow, mouth slightly open. And he sleeps; he is already fast asleep. Before his eyes, supposing that he forgot to close them, he can see an open balcony window. The evening breeze stirs the curtains which are not quite fully drawn and through the fluttering gap from time to time he can also see a roof quite far off and the summer sky over the town stretching northwards to the mountains. There's no more to say. Sleep, when it happens, is one of the simplest events imaginable.

He made a gesture of reproach. 'What silliness!' he said. Sleep may be called simple, but not everything simple in life can be made to correspond with sleep. Times when one has to stay up all night, for instance, even when purely a matter of form: vigils for the dead, these are simple enough or at least require a few words, for there's nothing you can say about someone dead apart from, 'He died, not me: he's the one who won't wake again!' The second half of this proposition, apparently so contradictory, is as much as to say: He is the one who'll never sleep again, not me, thereby nourishing the hope, no, the expectation of sleep to come.

He turned his back on the window: Bah! he said to himself, you don't have to be very smart to say such silly things and yet these simple interludes of desultory and facile thoughts are also called the dead hours. And these dead hours, he went on, are not only the hours of funeral wakes, but in general all hours of waiting, no matter what one is waiting for, even if it's nothing. In such cases it must be conceded that perhaps there is not such a great difference between waking and sleeping, but doubtless given the choice it's better to sleep stretched out in a good bed than waiting on a street corner with eyes wide open, as like as not in the rain.

'I repeat myself!' he grumbled. He realised that he was circling a confused memory, a blend of waking and sleeping: it is a silly memory, he told himself, a welter of problems and obscurities. Broadly speaking, he would describe it as a tortuous recollection of something like a general idea, always with different details, and each time incomplete: a print of a moonlit landscape depicting some unattainable mountainous place, a lamp, a half-open window. The right-hand side of each of these images seemed to be almost wholly obliterated, but even after long and hard scrutiny of the parts where something was legible he could never reach a conclusion, as though halted by a blank white stupor expanding over an inconceivable length of time.

'What are you waiting for?' they used to shout. 'Get lost, you're in the way!' and meekly he'd stand aside. He was not waiting, he was procrastinating, he would say to himself then, making distinctions like a clever child. In fact, whether he was hanging about or waiting, he wandered endlessly all over the house from the attics to the cellars, particularly in wintertime, silently or at most humming softly, so as to appear to be amusing himself. Or else, to keep up the pretence, he would steal off into the grey light of the cold rooms left to their long winter lethargy. He was hunting for sleep, he whispered as though the quest were somehow a perilous adventure through murky rooms full of shrouded mirrors and sofas and chairs cloaked in dusty sheets. Warily he would push through door after door toward the place where he would at last be able to sleep undisturbed, until bothered by so many creaky door hinges he gave up on his goal which almost out of spite grew more uncertain and futile each time he tried. By the light filtering through slats in the barred shutters over a double window he could make out a black and white moonlight landscape on one wall, which looked desolate, Japanese. Below it glowed the dull yellowish reflections of a brass lamp standing on a marble-topped chest; and glancing into the corner to his left he saw that the sheet covering a wicker chair had slipped to the floor to reveal, in the graceful curve of its arms and the placid sheen of faded silk, how easy it is to rest.

But then suddenly, alongside and inseparable from his perception of rest, as similar to rest as a synonym, he felt time slipping by, and the dead hour and so much, so very much silence already wasted. How would this waste ever end? he had wondered, while the grey scowling winter closed around him to prevent any escape.

He looked about him: even in this office now, had there been a comfortable and inviting armchair he might still have been tempted by the notion of rest, due to an ambiguity that at first sight made the ideas of rest and sleep appear complementary. Ambiguity, he now believed, is based on a process of approximation. Start by resting, you urge yourself, and the more you rest the nearer you get to an inertia as deep as sleep. In other words, you wait for sleep and meantime you struggle to be content with waiting, as though it were the very thing awaited. In this state of enforced indolence, a fatuous play of thoughts inevitably arises, vague resemblances between the most unlikely places start to occur, but in order to tolerate them you are forced to ignore differences and gloss over distinctions, set aside all verification, examination, evaluation – all analytic reasoning and thinking entirely. Without a thought in your head you lean back in your chair: through the half-open window you can make out a strip of countryside on the verge of summer with a few trees dotted about, silent and motionless. It's morning still: a morning without a lot of light, and a bit chilly despite the season. 'Relax!' you tell yourself. You look through the window with rigid gaze and in return everything you see seems to endorse your immobility. Nothing begins and nothing ends, and even if hour after hour every bell-tower marks the passing of time and possibly also the arrival of the future, this future meekly aligns itself with the present. In short, while awaiting sleep immobility prevails: a dense immobility stratified in numberless hours, bell-towers, future, and suchlike sound and fury. Perhaps rather than talking of present and future as different times, in this case it would be worth thinking of them as a process of oscillation, with everything now coming and now going, without really moving much. All that matters is the variation in proximity not only between the future and sleep but no end of other things, revealing likenesses between all of them which may indeed be provisional: at times futile and ridiculous, but at other times risky and wild as tigers at night. All in all, when we are asleep it is the similarities more than the differences between things that counts: in fact while sleeping we attend not to things but the similarities between things, or more generally the oscillations above and beyond the differences. When all is said and done, this last proposition might be a neat definition for sleep – but having thus defined sleep approximately and in theory, how does one actually get to sleep?

Maybe if I keep trying, perhaps resting my head on the desk, he pondered. He sat down, piled some paper up under one elbow and placed his head on top. Just for a start, he thought, I could begin with a proposition about this so-called oscillation or, better, swing.

'With a chin that sticks out like that,' his father said to his uncle, putting his gun in the gunrack, 'what kind of future can he have?' He shoved the two dogs out of the hall: 'Shoo, both of you,' he said with a scowl. 'They call him Chalky Chin, did you know that? Well, then let him do what he wants,' he went on, setting his cartridge belt down. Let him read Latin and even Greek if he likes ... Of course, he conceded after a short interval of unintelligible grumbles, you are right. I'll see he's taken to some whore. At least he'll learn how to use his prick.'

His first idea of the future came to him after this conversation as he squatted in the fork of the beech tree watching his father and his uncle through the open window. Obviously what the two were talking about was a future as minuscule and transient as the copper-coloured leaf before his eyes, but no less elegant. The whore they spoke of, for example, wasn't she perhaps futile and short-lived by definition? And yet, how seductive! Ah, the whore! he thought, seeing the foliage flutter in the breeze in the surrounding countryside. Whore, my little whorelet! he repeated to himself, almost singing out loud.

The wind grew stronger and the air filled with yellow leaves in flight, a joyous promise of the coming autumn. Everything promised a future close at hand: the sky empty of clouds was a presage of fresher winds and, almost part of this clarity and freshness, promised the whore to come with her soft gold and rosy skin. In these images or portents future and present resembled each other, interwoven like strands of moonlight on a prophetic night. *Oro y amor en la encendida noche* … And at that point he had dropped off to sleep and had fallen out of the tree with such a thud the dogs still running loose in the garden had rushed up to him.

And now, he said, raising his head from the reclining position which apart from anything else was rather uncomfortable, now fantasising about whores wouldn't put me to sleep even if I climbed to the top of a pine tree. The trouble was, he thought, that the future had become irrelevant for him, locked within a time that was not so much different from him as irremediably other than himself: a neutral time conventionally numbered. Is this the future? he had in fact asked himself when signing a lease for a store he owned in town and chanced to think of the years to come. His indifference to this future had nothing to do with the usual considerations about the futility or brevity of life or the dread of imminent death because being in good health for a man of thirty-five, he didn't see his own death as a likely occurrence. Strangely, though, while signing away what could be called a chunk of his own future in front of witnesses, he had felt this contractual future was a symptom of an extraneous eternity: image of oblivion, not of existence. But then where would the existence of the future be sought?

During his sleepless nights he had often struggled to seek out some prophecy or other sort of premonition, scanning the sky as the most probable location for portents, hunting for a signal that might betray the hidden and mysterious presence of things to come. It was not the mystery itself that he sought to unveil: he merely wanted to reassure or console his heart, and so sometimes even in the cold of autumn nights out on the open balcony for a better view, there was not a moonbeam gleaming on the rooftops or in the windows of the houses opposite, no branch stirring or other tiny detail however fleeting that he left unscrutinised. Every sudden downpour occasioned a persistent investigation of the future almost between one drop and the next. But no eventual future was ever in the signs.

I could get a chicken or rabbit gutted and inspect the intestines, he had thought once. So he went to an old woman in the countryside widely known for her ability to make remarkable predictions: 'Well, what do you want to know?' she asked. After some hesitation he had admitted there was nothing he wanted to know, and yet on hearing this the old woman refused to go on, sending him away with a haughtiness that approached disdain.

He grimaced with irritation. Forget it, he told himself. After all, the future, as it's commonly understood, is a preoccupation only for old witches. But what about the past? Did the past combine better with sleep, at least in the form of memories or even memories of a future? Because aside from precise expectations of specific events of a more or less agreeable nature, as in the episode of the first whore, there had indeed been moments in the past when he had had the premonition and almost the intimation of something to come and it had stayed with him always, no matter how hazy and indecipherable, instead of receding to become something else. There was, he had actually felt, even in the most seemingly negligible incidents, the close and palpable root of both what had been and of what was to come. It was, he would have said, what was immediate, the actuality of the present itself, or rather, without getting too long-winded, it could be said to be for instance the apple tree which two yards ahead of him seemed to have the look, the very pose, of the future, poised to bear apples not yet on its branches, and eventually to support them and proffer them with an affectionately pompous motion that presumes to provide nourishment: that self-important gesture which has not visibly altered since time immemorial. Therefore the future was not ensconced in barren distances beyond all reach, from whose remote brink even the most audacious fantasy can only peep into ever deeper vacancies, but much more humbly and so to say more frugally in this commonplace present moment restricted to the autumnal confines of a small patch of grass under the tender shadow of the apple tree. Such had been his enthusiasm that time he would have willingly taken over the tree, leaping feet first into its body and arboreal soul; but the tree had responded to his demented assault as if recoiling with grim and irreversible derision. It had been, he recalled, like reciting 'Oh my cypresses, my lovely little cypresses' and being applauded with a chorus of resounding farts.

That's how it goes! he said ruefully, shaking his head. More wisely now he restricted himself, at least in memory, to bidding the most restrained of farewells to the tree and his own dazzling future as an apple farmer. In fact the memory he now retained was indeed of the future, but in the sense of a future on the point of vanishing into the murk of as-it-was-so-it-must-be. In any case, so many objects, even the most humble in common use, which at one time or another in an instant of illumination had appeared to him to be lineaments of the future, stage-props for all his fantasies about what might come, due to some incomprehensible destiny of their own, on the edge of an ordinary day, sank from sight, and consigned to regret, that gloomy second-hand dealer in memory: a firescreen, a lamp, an empty bottle, *vieux flacon desolé,* fantasms now only wearily re-evoked, freshly dusted and sorted during the wait for sleep. Bric-a-brac so often revised, emended, re-edited, and so reworked by now that they were no longer capable of convincing anyone to expect anything. What indeed was to be expected in these dark times? Better to sleep.

And so the hunt for sleep continued, trailing a residue of frustrated somnolence: the memory of the past and that of the future (which in any case appeared explicitly only once, and, so to speak in *editio princeps,* in the apple tree) remained confined not so much to the world of memory as to the precious world of an authenticity now irretrievable, not least due to his confounded tendency to use words to keep afloat.

He stood up and started to pace up and down the room. 'Words!' he exclaimed, shaking his head and striking a pose midway between irony and disgust as best he could. 'Words!' he repeated to himself several times in the same tone. But every time he had to admit that these words had never let him down, and that actually he had used and abused them, riding on them towards his own caprices or sometimes following the caprices of the words, leaping in all directions by means of alliteration, metonymy and all the figures of speech that came into his head, sailing over a great swamp of silence. Without the buoyancy of words, unsteady and precarious as it was, that black swamp would have clasped him in its softness and he would have ended up completely, desperately alone. But then the clouds, the colours of the sky, the trees and leaves, the sand on the beaches, the rocks on the trails, the wheatfields, the crests of the hills in the distance... what would have become of all this?

'Ridiculous!' he said, shrugging his shoulders, There is no complaint a good sleep can't cure. Every problem for him was nothing but insomnia, but, as the doctors said, he was in excellent health and at some time or another he too would get a chance to sleep. In the meantime he cherished every detail of this future sleep with tireless imagination: the bed, the way the pillows were arranged, the light, the room temperature. Somewhere, he fancied, there was a room ideal for sleep: a place not necessarily very large, but silent and above all enclosed, walled on all sides so that the boredom and the clamour of the world could not intrude. Something modest which he could improve by buying a few things, perhaps even the broom cupboard or storeroom down the hallway from his office, for example, which he had once entered by mistake and which, revisited in his imagination, he thought he could easily equip for his purposes almost luxuriously, with at least a handsome deep armchair, if not a sofa, in addition to the bed. In any case the luxury was imprecise and the light dim: and yet the possibility of sleep in a such an odd place appeared more likely than in all the other rooms available to him, each being already tainted, so to speak, by an attempt to sleep and the consequent failure.

All the same, mulling over this eventual sleep and what practical steps he might take to gain it, he sometimes lost his way. Meandering through a maze of hypotheses and confutations, he came to an open place, a sort of concord of echoes at varying removes where things, though calling themselves by one name and then another maintained their distance and yet went forward together despite their casual or promiscuous verbal expression.

It might not be full sleep, but he felt he had attained a plausible imitation of it: it was roughly a not-feeling and yet recognising, a forgetting and yet remembering, and a knowledge mingled with ignorance. With such vague sophisms he alluded to a sleepless sleep similar to sailing on calm but unknown seas. There was the superb allure of an ocean-going vessel, but the grey of the calm sea gripped his heart; this oppressive calm, real though it was, often felt to him so laboured that his mind preferred to escape; and in an interminable dusk, swift as a rat, his memory scaled the steep ruins of his past constructions: words tumbled down from their ancient fixed positions creating a deliberately extravagant chatter. For example, seated on his bed, a wild crone looking like an aged dying aunt told tales about systems of priorities. According to her every unity was anchored to its own system of priorities which were not only moral but included grammar, syntax, even visual perception itself. Without this system, she maintained, nothing would manage to stand out from the common background; and it was, she added, a three-dimensional system and hence with a centre or a single priority above all others. For instance if bees set the greatest value on honey, then in their perception of the world each thing assumes its particular emphasis according to its distance and direction with respect to honey. This applies equally to people in various periods of history, assorted religions, different countries. Furthermore, this point of reference is a given fact: no one can choose a religion, a society, a country the way one selects a brand of toilet paper on a shelf in a store: 'My son,' she finally implored him after her long peroration, 'if the shit is rising in this country it is because shit has the highest value. Therefore, I beg you, give shit top priority in all your thoughts and you will lead a useful and honourable life.' She ended her sermon by releasing a huge fart, vanishing beyond all the fog of the visible. But this speech furnished him with no light, nor any benefit, for it seemed to him that all things even when subordinated to shit still remained the same, indifferent and in fact irrelevant, entangled in an ubiquitous shitty background from which he struggled to extricate them in vain. 'Piss,' he asked himself, 'would piss be better?' And he tried without success to imagine the country as a lagoon of piss. But how could he decide which was better or worse?

He returned to his desk slowly and composed himself in a dignified manner. 'So which is better,' he repeated, 'shit or piss?' As a matter of fact he had never contemplated judgements of such vast consequence because he lived his daily life amidst opinions and passions, concerning himself with the immediate and the transitory, while solemn decisions about what was better or worse for the country required a robust conscience and consequently absolute faith in one's own arguments: a faith uncluttered by passing emotions. And if his own life as he had lived it could be called deprived or at least poor in emotional content, this poverty was not the result of choice but of chance. In other words, he had never abstracted his own individual will from existence in general and therefore it would have been inappropriate or even irreverent to contemplate the destiny of the country so to speak on equal terms, shitty or pissy as it might be.

'Forget it!' he resolved, striking the desk with his fist and making the papers shake. But if he could not sleep or live sleeping as he stubbornly tried to do, in the absence of great choices or grand subjects or themes, what was to be done with his consciousness? Where could he place his own undeniable awareness of living?

'Let's imagine ...' he said to himself, leaning back in his chair. 'Let's just relax and imagine, for example, that one winter night a traveller arrives in some unknown town intending to stay there: let's say it's this very town with its ephemeral inhabitants, provisional and interchangeable: men and whores who meet only once because even if they were to meet again they wouldn't recognise each other, or even the town, strangers by definition. Town and inhabitants and houses and streets, therefore, of an unawareness so exemplary as to merit inclusion in the sophistic lists: a sad grey ignorance with no escape, for which living could only be resignation.

He closed his eyes, trying to imagine this sadness in a way both practical and even wise, like the pursuit of humble virtues and the satisfaction of faded pleasures: a tree-lined street in summer, a flat not too spacious, a not unattractive woman. In thrall to this fantasy of a minimal life, behind his eyelids he conjured light and dark, reflections and colours: all those elements of sight which bring life to even the haziest images without being anything in themselves: a woman never seen, an unknown street, a house never lived in. Evanescent phantoms of which the house was possibly the most enduring: empty of people perhaps, but at least furnished with beds and chairs and tables: the solitude of things under the tireless surveillance of polished mirrors.

But how long could he live in this house of fantasy, opening and closing unknown doors, watching the rustle of the trees outside the panes in non-existent windows? He glanced at his watch: time seemed to trickle by with implacable slowness, the hours just didn't manage to fill up with all the minutes and seconds assigned to them, except with the greatest effort. Time seemed to advance undecided, at times even seemed tempted to go into reverse.

'Away!' he exhorted himself. 'The answer is to get far away.' That is, he urged himself to flee the obsessive slowness of local time, to head for a sky with swifter clouds, a light more quick to be born and die. Because here instead the light showed no sign of wanting to leave the summit of the sky. Perhaps, as sometimes happens at sunset, the sky was immobilised in long strips of tranquil clouds behind which the sun stagnated or perhaps, under cover of these long shadows, was now mounting the sky again to go back over its previous journey.

He stopped, closing his eyes with a smile midway between disdain and self-pity. At times he was so indignant with himself that he would have gladly beaten himself with a club. Instead he limited himself to a few clouts, not hitting himself, which would be silly as well as difficult, but surprising the first person he saw and whacking him over the ears, making a great deal of noise but causing little harm, he trusted. In any case the hullabaloo that followed calmed him and reduced his self-indignation to a milder inward laugh. Certainly there was no generosity or even elegance in these practical jokes played on his unsuspecting fellow man; but who would ever maintain that a game has to be either magnanimous or elegant?

Also this assault on a fellow human being gave him, at least fleetingly, the consolation of not being alone. The other person in other words, wasn't only his neighbour because of the generic similarity, but was almost himself by proxy, standing in to receive the clout intended for himself. So, for the duration of a minute or two this kinship cancelled his solitude, and along with the solitude, the grouchiness that typifies solitary people. Moreover, perhaps some of his blows were delivered not only out of rage at himself but also because at times after a particularly resounding thump over the back of a head he could sense his victim's heart swelling with a confused but violent desire for war. The hope, that is, if not for machine-guns firing in the main square, at least a few gunshots in the streets, which would undeniably have made life in the land more interesting, and certainly more dignified.

The door which at that moment he happened to be watching began to open silently and imperceptibly. When it had reached a sufficient width, this silent opening produced in no time as if by magic a complete woman, five foot seven inches tall, nimble and light, who appeared to be more old than young, that is his secretary in person.

'Good for you!' he laughed. 'Is that the way you appear before me when I'm least expecting you?'

She lowered her eyes with a deliberately childish show of vexation: 'I can't always do it,' she murmured, and closing the door behind her moved towards him with an air of conspiracy. From under raised eyebrows she inspected him with wide-open enormous eyes, slow and glowing like those of a beast in the dark, while her mouth, which was naturally large with generous lips, pouted to suggest secrecy in a way that was explicitly charged and clownish. In any case, as every afternoon, her entrance signalled for him a sudden passage from a situation which was, so to speak, silent if not quiet to another which was agitated and noisy, even if more full of whispers than sounds. On second thoughts, the passage or rather leap was in language, that is from the silence of a language that was strictly only thinkable to the noise or rather verbalism of the language in everyday usage: that in which a single word, for example 'crap', variously conjugated (take, talk, eat) designates the entire range of interpersonal relationships possible in the country.

Without hesitation therefore he exclaimed: 'Do me a favour! Go and get stuffed!' while not concealing his affection for the woman; in fact smiling at her.

'I already have!' she reassured him, this time with a cordial urgency. 'Now you please do me a favour!' she went on, lowering her voice. 'Don't smile. It's alarming to see a smile on a face like yours. I'm always afraid that all that weight could make the lower part of your face drop off.'

They both laughed mildly. 'Oh, yes,' he resumed. 'You can joke ... As if I had time to waste on your silliness. I have problems of my own, I have!'

She nodded several times, encouragingly.

'Hmm,' he continued. 'My main problem, my true problem is that I can't ever get to sleep.'

She took hold of a chair on the other side of the desk and sat down: 'Would you like me to tell you a dream?' she proposed.

'Yes, do sit down, do sit down,' he invited her. 'Let's see. What dream do you want to tell me this time?'

'An easy one,' she said, and her face brightened. 'So easy in fact that even you could have it.' She paused, looking up from under her eyelashes. 'Let's try this,' she went on. 'Word went round that the sun was entirely covered with little crosses and the old women swore that this was a bad omen.'

'What sun? What old women? What little crosses? What sort of story is this?' he asked, laughing.

'It's a story within a dream,' she explained patiently, tracing the edge of the desk with her fingers spread. 'Now I say "sun" but in the dream this word refers to nothing, merely indicates a possibility. What's more, all the words of the dream are words for show: one says "sun" and sees the sun with bare eyes, or actually one sees it as a painted disk rather than a blinding light. In other words in the dream the sun has a moderate brightness, but more visible than usual; and therefore better for interpretation because in the dream everything that can be seen is part of a possible interpretation. Hermeneutics are the law, and therefore since the phrase "little cross" (whether someone actually said it or for some other reason) occurred in the context of "sun", from the point of view of interpretation at least it could be accepted that the sun was covered with little crosses. I didn't see them, but I was willing to believe people who claimed to see them. Is it clear now?'

'Go on,' he said. 'I'm interested.'

'Well now,' she went on, 'a great fog rolled in and in a corner of this fog, near the bell tower, an old woman was wailing and shaking her head: "How badly I've been fucked! All my life they fucked me badly." "How did that happen?" I asked "Who fucked you so badly?"

'And she: "All those fat-cats: they overeat and that brings on a bestial lust, because, as St. Jerome said *venter et genitalia sunt sibi propinqua ut ex vicinitate membrorum colligatur confoederatio vitiorum*. Or as it is put more simply in the Psalms: *Prodit quasi ex adipe iniquitas eorum*. Therefore, these fat-cats are always trouble, though often their pricks are limp."'

'That's certainly true,' he agreed. 'This part about the fat-cats I like. But could you please explain it word for word, as you did before?'

'Oh, no!' she exclaimed. 'It's not possible to tell a dream and at the same time distract oneself with explanations. Every dream is its own interpretation. So if you want me to tell them to you, you must be happy with what I say.'

'So be it!' he accepted. 'And by the way,' he added, 'when you tell your dreams you even look pretty.'

She thanked him for the compliment with a nod of her head. 'So,' she continued, 'while the old woman went on bewailing her lot, some shrill and confused voices could be heard in the air above the houses, with no sign of whoever was making these sounds. The fog thickened, wrapping all the daylight in a whiteness so thick you could stroke it, while all around hens and roosters kept clucking and crowing. Convinced that this racket from the poultry yards announced the Last Judgement, a lot of people armed themselves with clubs to hit the authorities over the head and brain them. At this point I hid, that is I took the old woman *mal baisée* by the arm and we went together looking for a latrine. At least that's the way it seemed.'

'Go on,' he said, 'go on with the story.'

'Ah,' she laughed, 'it's not worth it! And then to go on from here I would lapse into propaganda; there would be no more wonder or surprise, but at best one would be entertained by the spectacle of the dream, because at this point the dream has already declared its theme or at least revealed its thesis, which is politics in this case. There were men armed with clubs and you can well understand their intentions.'

'Oh, really,' he observed with irritation. 'How can you be so sure?'

She half smiled, but remained silent.

'It is not the least bit easy,' he continued. 'I certainly couldn't have such a dream. And you, when did you have it? Last night? The night before? Monday?'

'There are no dates in dreams. And if there were they would be forgotten, because days are all alike when one is dreaming. And then, even awake, you, for example, do you always know what day of the week it is?'

He made an evasive gesture and getting up from his desk, went towards the window. Looking into the courtyard, into the almost liquid shadow it contained, he felt he was gazing at the image of a previous day, Thursday which was yesterday, or another day before that, perhaps Monday. All he could say was that this hypothetical Monday was lying around now in various parts of the courtyard, certainly transparent, but only just a little bit colder and slightly more opaque than the present day. Perhaps, he thought, this frail remnant of the past was no more than the ghost of the stillness of the courtyard, the spectre of the grey stone, of its thickness and weight in columns arches and cornices: and this stagnating phantom of architecture, shadow in the shadow, resembled the ghostly illusion or simple desire for sleep that he uselessly pursued day after day, Thursdays, Wednesdays, and Mondays too.

He heard the rustle of pages. 'She'll be wanting to tidy up' he thought. Instead, a moment later his secretary started speaking again a bit dreamily about the days of the week. 'Friday,' she was saying, 'what does Friday mean? And Saturday? For me these nouns all evoke images of a swing.'

'Yes,' he said. 'It could be. What's more,' he added after a while, 'dreams in themselves don't interest me. They simply indicate sleep. That's all. If I remember a dream I can assume I have been asleep, as when one says: "If she has milk, she has given birth".'

The comparison pleased him and he started to laugh.

She watched him stupefied: 'You know,' she said, 'you remind me of one of my classmates? When we were both fourteen years old he was talking about the Stoics which he found amusing, while I was thinking: My God, how young he is!'

He started to laugh again. 'You,' he said, 'were not thinking then: "My God, how young he is!" but rather: "To hell with him, how stupid he is!" otherwise the similarity to me would not have crossed your mind.'

She looked at him for a while without responding. 'I feel at ease with you,' she eventually said, 'as if we were classmates. Despite the socio-economic difference, I am sure the two of us can laugh at the same things, with no disrespect on my side.'

'And why should you show respect for me?' he asked. 'Never, never do that!' he pleaded. 'Besides, it is in the finest tradition to be disrespectful when one speaks of dreams.'

'We are not only talking about dreams,' she retorted. 'You

yourself have already acknowledged that at times I have given you some interesting information.'

He nodded.

'So,' she went on, 'as you already know, this New Finance syndicate that concerned itself with advances on bribes and recycling of anomalous sums, at least officially (that is, for all they tell me) now has extended its activity to life annuities.'

'That I know,' he said crossly. 'What's new about that?'

'Private,' she whispered, 'Private news, this time. It concerns my father. I've received a letter of congratulation because my father has supposedly expressed an intention to take out a life annuity.'

'Why should New Finance congratulate you,' he asked, making an effort to show surprise. 'After all, it is contrary to his personal interest.'

'It is a way like any other to warn me,' she replied. 'But surely you understand more than you want me to believe! No? And yet you know the man very well. All right, let's forget about it! What bothers me is that in the last two months, the syndicate has issued about fifty life annuities. Unfortunately not many of the beneficiaries of these policies are still alive today. Some fell from balconies, some slipped and banged their heads on a step. The old pharmacist on the Corso drowned in his bath and the man who sold stamps in via dell'Orso fell from the top of the tower of Porta Vecchia in the middle of the night: at two in the morning, they say. There is more than one reason to be superstitious, wouldn't you agree?'

'What can I say?' he replied brusquely. 'Why mix me up in it? That character you are alluding to, I have only seen him twice and only on official occasions. And then I am not in business with anyone. I have never had anything to do with politicians, not me. Everything I own I inherited and I can prove that down to the last penny.'

'Of course, of course!' she assured him. 'This is also well known. And yet the fact remains that some people in town as rich or even richer than you are now either dead or living in the direst poverty; but you are in good health and still hold onto all your patrimony.'

'What is that supposed to imply?' he demanded, banging his fist on the desk.

'Come on,' she laughed, 'Why take it like that? I merely wanted to say that there is no longer any distinction between money and politics and that by now wherever there is money there must be politics, or as they say: *qui tangit picem, inquinabitur ab ea.*'

He got up from the desk.

'Are you an agent provocateur now?' he asked with affected gentleness. 'Who told you to come here to disturb me?' Without waiting for a reply, he turned his back on her and walked away. 'Silly chatterbox!' he said as if to himself. 'Even as a spy she's not worth much.'

'You're afraid!' she commented.

He turned and reached her almost in one bound.

'You don't mean to hit me, do you?' she asked, standing up so swiftly that the chair toppled over on the carpet.

He stopped himself at once: 'Perhaps,' he said, 'I don't always weigh my words, but have you ever heard anyone say I ever struck a woman?'

'No?' she asked with diffidence, while she righted the chair. They eyed each other for a few moments; then, as if in agreement, both sat down again.

'Why do you say so many silly things?' he resumed. 'Haven't I always been civil with you, whenever I had occasion?'

She nodded. 'I'm afraid,' she said. 'I too have always been very afraid. It would be stupid not to admit it: you can read it in my face! At the beginning it wasn't that way, don't you remember? We opened the newspapers and read about bribes and graft. We shrugged our shoulders: it wasn't our money. Then came the kidnapping and extortion. "Just four scoundrels!" we said and still shrugged our shoulders. How long ago? Ten years? Twenty? Twenty years ago I was writing my thesis. I ended up with honours for my academic labours and, when the time came to compete for jobs, I had to admit that the scoundrels were neither four nor forty, but at least forty million! How many fucks in exchange for vague promises! So, screw today, screw tomorrow, I eventually got my job too and so I began screwing my way up. It seems only yesterday doesn't it? You certainly didn't have to follow my curriculum. You jumped straight to the top of the hierarchy, five years ago, one fine spring day. Your predecessor had shot himself three times in the head. There were so many suicides at that time. In any case no one was surprised when you arrived. They said you inherited not only his beautiful house on the Corso, the shops under the porticos and who knows what else, but also certain documents deposited in solid foreign safes. "Won't those documents ever expire?" a lot of people are now asking themselves.'

While she was speaking he shook his head in a manifestly pitying way though she couldn't see him because she stubbornly kept her gaze fixed on her hands, in fact inspecting them with a frown: 'Rubbish!' he finally said, displaying more boredom than anger in his voice.

'Do I bore you?' she asked, suddenly looking him straight in the face with her large eyes wide open.

He smiled and returned to pitying mode: 'I am sorry,' he said. 'You are clearly upset, but I don't understand why you feel such rancour.'

'Rancour?' she protested. 'Certainly not. Every one knows you are harmless, aside from a few punches. I actually feel sorry for you. When those documents of yours expire what will happen to you? Will you defend yourself with punches?'

'So you feel sorry for me?' he laughed. 'You really aren't being very nice to me today.'

'All right! I'm out of my mind. Try to forgive me. What do you recommend?'

'Hmm,' he said with evident hesitation. 'What do I know about your doings?' He didn't want to appear to be too rude, however. 'After all,' he added, 'You know what they want. I don't.'

'According to me,' she said, moving closer to him confidingly, 'it is a piece of land in the country we have above the road to the lighthouse. About eight acres in all. A conservation zone: no buildings of any sort allowed there, not even a hut, but 'they', I am told, have already been granted planning permission for a big hotel. If I let them have it, do you think they will let me keep the flat in town?'

He looked at her for a full minute without responding, but the questioning tension in her face did not diminish.

'I don't see why not,' he finally said. 'After all a three-room flat in an old building, as you have described it to me, isn't even worth the cost of a notary in these cases.'

'That sounds right,' she nodded. 'You've made me feel much better. After all, little people like us have always been left more or less in peace. It's the hotel they're after. Perhaps I could even squeeze a bit of money out of it. What do you say?'

'Why not?' he encouraged her. 'Give it a try!'

'Can I use your name?' she asked. 'You know, just drop it into the conversation. After all I am your secretary.'

'I am not a good reference,' he said. 'You acknowledged that yourself.' He stood up and paced the room, waving a hand as though to chase off something bothersome. 'And then,' he added, 'it is not elegant to get mixed up in other people's affairs.' He tried to laugh without success.

A long silence followed. He went to the window, pretending to study something in the courtyard. 'And yet,' he said after a while, 'if you think my name could be of use ...'

'I would do it just ...' she excused herself, 'in a symbolic sense, more to reassure myself than to intimidate or persuade them.'

They both fell silent.

'In a symbolic sense?' he asked without looking at her, after more than a minute.

'I,' she said, 'when I am really afraid I start chattering at random to keep from crying, and also say things off the top of my head. For instance, I mention names of people who have nothing to do with it, neither with the facts, nor with me: names of people I have never fucked. It's like turning to some saint, I suppose, to tear my eyes off the shit that terrifies me. Diversionary names, let's say that I pompously call symbolic just to sound intellectual. Weren't we taught from the most tender age that the property of symbols is that they are "other" with respect to any context whatsoever? Symbols, we were told, are not topics but absolutes, and therefore, paradoxically, are available for the most risky combinations like cabbages at teatime. Well, no matter what you say, I don't feel I have been discourteous, saying that I hoped to use your name symbolically.'

There was a fresh silence.

'And do the big-bellies have a symbolic function?' he finally asked, conciliatingly.

'You mean in my dream?' she asked in her turn. 'Did you like it?'

'Yes, amusing,' he admitted. 'That is, what you have to say about symbols is amusing. And I think the same can be said of dreaming, even of sleep. Perhaps we no longer know how to speak according to the old ways and traditions, instead we dream – at least those of us who can. Rhetoric is finished and now symbols are all the rage: when rhetoric's day is over, barbarism begins. Don't you agree? I would prefer simply to sleep.'

'Rhetoric!' she said with sudden warmth. 'Think of the way good composition was taught twenty years ago. In chorus the teachers used to chant: *jubent exordiri...deinde rem narrare... post autem dividere causam...Tum alii conclusionem orationis collocant, alii jubent ante quam peroretur, digredi.*'

'All right,' he interrupted her. 'But look at this courtyard. At certain moments I don't recognise it.'

He went on watching the shadow that coated the walls of the courtyard with the oppressive sensation of never having seen it before: 'Extraordinary,' he finally exclaimed aloud for the surprise. 'But this is sleep!' That is, the courtyard as a whole, not in any precise point, had suddenly appeared to him to be sleep in person, with the demeanour of sleep and all the features of sleep clearly legible. Certainly to see sleep right before your eyes was one thing and to enjoy it another; but however intangible, sleep had never been so close to him and it unsettled him. 'I saw it!' he said to himself and the fact that now, no matter how hard he tried, he could not manage to see it any longer did not diminish his excitement and sense of gratitude, because now he felt he could speak of it with understanding and almost from experience.

'I know what sleep is like,' he declared.

'Ah!' she said, 'Your mania for sleep!'

'What could be better? Sleep is beautiful, restful, and I would even say wholly satisfying. Don't you think so?' He moved closer to her, and placing a hand on her shoulder went on to talk about sleep, citing examples from the past as well: sleeps like gardens of shadows without any plot or content describable, like when he was a boy and one afternoon in open country he fell asleep watching the tall poplars full of little leaves ever more luminous, ever more tiny and at the very tips sinking into the depths of the sky. Finally he also cited more recent sleeps, winter ones, half inventing the circumstances.

'And so,' he ended, 'sometimes I too have happened to sleep, naturally almost without being aware of it. What about you?'

She nodded: 'That's how it happens, just as you say. Rhetoric is finished.' She continued, as if trying hard to find the words: 'Once rhetoric was everywhere. Remember? In songs, speeches, in the first timid approaches between boys and girls. And then the great love, the grand passion, the great challenge of life which we imagined hazily (but with grand words resounding with imperatives) would resolve everything in a grand victory for rhetoric. All gone! There are merely ghosts now in a labyrinth of regrets and we have nothing more to resolve. The weight of all that remains unresolved seems pathetic to us and even breaks our balls. This is the truth! Everything begins from nothing and without warning ends in nothing,' she said, shaking her head and as if talking to herself.

He was silent for a while. 'Anyhow,' he said in the end grumpily, 'you don't even listen to me. Yet you come asking me for advice or rather to irritate me. Now I'm tempted to think someone sent you to tell me your nonsense. Out of curiosity? For a joke?'

'No, no!' she protested, taking his hand and holding it between hers. 'Don't say things like that. On the contrary, I am grateful to you. Don't you believe me?'

He shrugged his shoulders, placated, trying to extricate his hand without seeming too brusque. He moved away from her chair. 'Why do we have to quarrel? But it is actually quite amusing' he said, and started to laugh.

'It's the fault of the fat-cats!' she laughed in turn. 'As you see, I feel like the old woman in my dream. But truly don't you also think that things would go better if we had people in power who were not so fat and not such gluttons? These big-bellies bring bad luck, in my opinion.'

'Well, well! And how so?' he asked.

'I don't know,' she replied, making a fanning motion with her hand. 'Among other things I imagine them always surrounded by a dense stink of farts. When I saw you right up close to the character who proposed the life annuity I thought: 'Won't he be gassed?'

He made a gesture of irritation.

'Go ahead and laugh,' he said. 'Do you think you are so smart? So intelligent? Do you think you can get away with it, by laughing along with everyone else or am I the only clown for you?'

'All right,' she said, dropping her head. She stood up, but then hesitated, with her hand on the back of the chair. 'You see,' she said, 'I must confess I sometimes feel nostalgia for elevated language. Now, for example, if I could unbare my heart I would take flight on wings of poesy to express my thanks. But today with the feet of the big-bellies planted on our hearts, how can we use those lofty expressions that not so long ago we at least heard at the opera? Their great big feet have trampled on our elevated words, the tragic and even the comic. Nevertheless I thank you with tears in my eyes. I even kiss your hand. Would you like a kiss on the hand?'

He shook his head without saying anything and continuing to watch her, sunk into herself now and almost clinging to the chair, weary with the weight of her forty years, while the silence grew, almost to the point of passing from silence into emptiness. Finally he managed to take his eyes off her and look over to the window still benignly filled with afternoon light, while she began to speak again: this time, as was her wont, her tone was at times almost theatrically solemn and yet voluble, but always with transparent traces of her customary mocking humour.

'I want to tell you another dream,' she said, 'not an easy one like the first, but curious. And then, who knows, perhaps you will manage to resolve it in a way different from mine. It involved a fortified structure and a courtyard: something square and dim without being truly dark. In fact there is a lamp somewhere; the light comes at strange angles. Perhaps it's not that structure; perhaps it is more accurate to say that as I dream I am in the grip of an oppressive feeling: heaviness, a sort of walled-in feeling and I am trying to explore this feeling word by word. I go from one word to another and go blindly, but with some hope of a solution, until this feeling closes in front of me, hemming me in like a blank wall. But this is the point: this hemming in (I think still in the dream) perhaps is not a failure, but actually the solution. What do you think?'

'What solution?' he asked, to be polite. Her chatter no longer interested him. What's more, he feared her words concealed some trap. She can take good care of herself, after all, he thought bitterly.

'Well,' she said, 'it is more a hypothesis, or rather a hint of a solution; perhaps it is barely a word, but the last, the one word remaining after all those through which I passed in order to arrive at that wall. If you promise me not to laugh, I will tell you.'

'Go ahead, tell me!' he grumbled. He moved away, turning his back on her and starting to look out of the window again.

'All right,' she said to his back, lowering her voice. 'The word is God. Of course,' she continued hesitantly, 'in saying God I realise that the expression sounds incongruous, to say the least. A structure, a wall is God? you will say. But what sort of simile is this? What metaphor? All right, I say. This is a concrete, small God, that's understood; not the immensity of grace, nothing bigger than a falcon God who can swoop down on the big-bellies and rip them open. But apart from this blasphemous reduction of divinity, in the face turned towards them, in the more ample face, even if this too is reductive, in the wall that I see or rather grope to touch, there is also something solid for me: a wall smooth as jasper, very tall, forming a barrier against malevolent stars. Of course I use the word wall just to name something real, but I believe that the names of actual things, even taken at random, if said of God, always bring a sort of idolatrous peace, a pagan consolation, but so persuasive I could weep.'

'But what kind of wall?' he asked, under his breath.

The light seemed to darken by half a tone. A passing cloud, he said to himself; but he felt oppressed: shadows, clouds, lights, whatever they were, all things visible appeared to be heading more intently towards desolation now.

'How can I put it?' she laughed. 'With this bad habit of symbols, today we think we have the power to summon everything into our presence and resolve everything in the midst of our own mess, including God, while actual things taken one by one, the names of realities, at least, are like destiny: unexpected they rear up before our ignorance, and sometimes unexpectedly they can seem to us to be the solution. This is when we are dreaming, of course. Isn't that why you are searching for dreams?'

'No,' he said. 'I am not searching for dreams. And then what solution are you going on about?'

They were both silent for a moment. 'All right,' he said, 'but now you should go.'

'Should I say that I'll let them have the land at a good price?' she asked timidly.

'Of course,' he approved. 'But now go and get stuffed, if you please.'

'Right away!' she whispered. And with a rustle she was gone, leaving the scene empty, he felt, with theatrical suddenness.

All the same, the office was and remained, as always, modern and comfortable: the bare walls, the mild temperature, the silence and, in the distance, the hum of typewriters, the light and the day slowly slipping towards sunset evoked the idea of sleep again with renewed dignity. The courtyard too, now distinctly narrow yet grandiose, seemed to be made of the same unalterable and infinite substance as the shadow. A reticent day was retreating: there were columns and arches and paving stones; there was shadow everywhere and in the shadow the serenity that prevailed was that peculiar to farewells and the renunciation of those who know they are sleeping.

# DEAD HOURS

The old man had stopped him on the stairs: 'Sometime I'd like to have a few words with you!'

'A few?' he had asked.

'I mean have a coffee together,' the other persisted. 'Whenever you like'.

'Why not now?' he suggested. So they had set off for a cafe.

The day had been bright because of the strong north wind. Now that the wind had dropped the light was steady, but the sky was not settled. He was walking beside the old man along a quiet side-street, unable to take his mind off the celestial restlessness. Something on high was moving and yet not moving: it was, he decided, the firm strength of the sky behind the subtle chill in the air and the pale tones and shadowy transparencies that seemed to harbour possibilities of metamorphosis, as mighty as ocean tides: an expert eye, a mariner's for instance, could have discerned hints and intimations here and there, faint flashes of what was to come.

'Isn't it beautiful?' he asked, pausing to sniff the air.

The other, who was a pace ahead, turned to look at him and shook his head. Luckily the cafe they had in mind was not far. Turning a corner, they found themselves in a road that was very short yet broad and lined with trees: more a widening than a true street. A lone remnant of some town planner's short-lived dream, cut off from traffic in the middle of a quarter full of narrow dark alleys, this surviving sample of the frenzy for demolition that now already seemed so long ago always gave him an eerie feeling. Although still in good condition, the buildings looked as desolate as discarded stage-sets, the trees had too many branches, the shop windows were too big and clean, and the windows in the upper stories above the treetops were even more stagey, vast gleaming panes mirroring the furthest pallor of the sky.

'I have never liked this place' he commented, pausing again.

'Well,' the other said, 'if we don't like it we'll have to go all the way to the Caffé della Posta which is always full even at this time of day.'

He looked around undecided. Apart from the haberdasher and an ironmonger the shutters were down on the shops along the forty yards of pavement between them and the cafe. Across the street the bakery looked deserted, while it was impossible to see into the other two shops because their windows were full of objects with no criteria to their arrangement other than membership of the same family or species of thing: the family of locks and door bolts in one and that of stockings and underwear in the other.

They went in and sat at a table towards the back of the cafe, looking out at the immobile branches of the trees through the window. Aside from the waiter, who came towards them immediately, the cafe was deserted and so silent that they instinctively lowered their voices.

'Is it true you spent a long time in the North?' the other asked.

He nodded with irritation, while spontaneously and inevitably his memory replayed the ashen image of the northern province where he had lived for a few years. The old man, he decided, was disagreeable. What did he want to talk about?

'You were good at sport, they tell me,' the man continued. 'With your height and physical strength, I'm surprised that you didn't become a champion: famous, I mean. Or were you famous?'

'Oh, no,' he protested. 'I wouldn't even call it sport ... just a bit of exercise to keep fit.'

The other spread his arms: 'Fame is fickle.'

He made no comment.

As they drank their coffee in silence he noticed that the other, despite his potbelly and fleshy shoulders, had a bony face, almost sunken-cheeked. His eyes were deep-set on either side of a large nose beneath a hard jutting forehead. His skull, bald on top, was similarly composed of harsh angles, covered by pink skin mottled with darker patches. 'He is sixty years old,' he recalled, and even the man's age struck him as objectionable.

'A young fellow like you,' the other resumed, 'has many opportunities for notoriety, if not for fame, even here.'

The old man fell silent for a minute or two, and finding himself calmly left to his silence, he sighed and added: 'Good opportunities and others not so good.'

'Why the sigh?' he asked.

The old man gestured towards the window. 'I used to live in that house,' he said. 'Someone used to repair bicycles in the courtyard. I was thirty years old then.'

'I believe it,' he assured him. And he turned around to watch the waiter behind him straighten the cloth on the neighbouring table.

'You may wonder why I wanted a word with you,' the other said. Receiving no reply, he went on: 'Your habit of going round hitting people is drawing unwanted attention to the provincial departments. "Provincial functionaries beat people up" they're saying, making no distinction between the various offices. One man actually asked me: "Are you the beater-up?" and I had to explain to him that I was in statistics and not in the cultural department.'

'If he was looking for a punch,' he interrupted, 'you should have directed him straight to me.'

'Of course,' the other conceded. 'Very true. In any case, most people are better informed. Actually, what is famous is you, not your department; so if anyone muddles the two it is from sheer malice.'

'And that worries you?' he asked.

The old man stirred his empty cup with his spoon. 'Worry me?' he asked. And without waiting for an answer added, 'Wouldn't you like an aperitif?'

He shook his head, but then changed his mind: 'Let's have a bottle of wine,' he suggested. 'You see,' he explained, 'I can't stand aperitifs.'

'At four o'clock?' the other exclaimed.

'An excellent time,' he said. 'Anyhow I drink every Friday and today happens to be a Friday ...'

'White wine then?' the man proposed.

'If that's what you like.'

'It's not exactly that I like it,' the other man said, scratching the backs of his hands distractedly, 'but since it is Friday .... '

They ordered a bottle of the best and later, having established that even a white can be a good wine, ordered a second.

'Believe me,' said the old man, pressing a hand to his heart in token of his sincerity. 'All these beatings I hear about intrigue me partly because I must confess I'm a bit envious: If I don't like someone's face, wham! If I don't care for someone's tone of voice, pfaff! That'll shut you up! Why did I never think of it, I've sometimes wondered. Because you know when I was thirty I was quite a hunk myself, although certainly not in your class. All the same,' he went on after a pause, 'this meeting of ours is not on my own initiative. I was asked to take it on. "You are the oldest," they told me, "you are the most senior." And they badgered me so much that I resigned myself to taking up a little of your time.'

'Never mind' he commented politely.

'To take up a little of your time, as I was saying. I was so curious to see you at close range that I said to myself: "All right, let's carry out this mission": the one assigned to me, I mean.'

'What mission is that?' he asked.

'It is and is not a mission,' he replied. 'Perhaps, with all due respect, it is an investigation. In other words, it is what we'd like to know without disturbing you too much.'

'Investigation?' he asked. But he didn't wait to hear the reply. Instead he summoned the waiter and ordered two more coffees.

'Let's get things straight,' he proceeded. 'In the case of an investigation it is always best.'

And while the other apologised for using the expression 'investigation', which was simply meant to be a precaution and in no way alarming, he decided to say nothing. Let's see what this nasty old man is after, he said to himself. Anyhow the coffee immediately following the wine clarified his thoughts or at least induced a sort of calm detachment, so he could listen to the old man without excessive irritation. He is just babbling! he soon decided and stopped paying attention.

On the other side of the cafe window he had before his eyes a tree that rose black and leafless from the pavement, and through its branches he could see the house and trees across the street, immersed in a steady light without a hint of evening. And yet, he thought, it will soon be dusk. The sun sets fast in winter. But the tree remained immobile in its lines, without the slightest change of hue, and this stillness of the tree also seemed to stall time itself in an interval of happy duration. And then when night comes it too will be accepted without fuss. That's all, he thought with admiration.

'Well?' he asked, just to say something, since the old man had now stopped talking.

'Well, yes indeed,' the other said with that peremptory manner which drunks suddenly adopt when they don't feel understood. 'Yes indeed!' he repeated stubbornly, pouring himself another glass from the bottle which was still half full.

He nodded. But since the fellow was eyeing him questioningly, not knowing what to say he indicated the tree outside the window: 'Do you know that tree gives me a feeling of serenity?'

The other glanced at the tree and then back at him: 'It doesn't look properly pruned to me,' he said in a voice that had become completely calm again.

He admitted this might be the case, and they dropped the subject of the tree. The old man is drunk, he thought, and like all drunks tends to believe that I am too. So much the better! he decided. In any case, what could he have said about any tree that would be comprehensible to anyone with such an angular head? And then, he thought with sudden annoyance, these beautiful people have the nerve to talk about my lantern jaw! He shook his head resolutely, almost to shake off his irritation.

The old man chuckled: 'You ought to be careful when you move your head, because anyone in the way of that jaw of yours could get flattened. Far worse than a punch!'

'I'll be careful,' he assured him. 'But since you are such a witty companion, why don't we drop the formalities and drink another bottle together, possibly a rather better one?'

'Amen to that!' the old man agreed, with a hint of a bow, and very soon the waiter arrived with a new bottle ceremoniously wrapped with a napkin at its neck.

But aren't feelings strange! he thought to himself. The old man irritated him to the point that he could have happily punched him; and yet he had to admit that at times he was almost entertaining. Since childhood he had worried about this tendency feelings have to contradict each other, muddle and merge, so much that one night the notion had come to him that it would be so much easier to keep them distinct if they were each allocated a visibly different place: shady or sunny, dark and leafy or else parched and thorny, using the variety of nature in a metaphoric way. So he had begun calling the passions no longer by their usual names, such as anger, calm, sadness, but by the names of nearby villages that he knew had been planted firmly on the hills since time immemorial: Perdeterra, Salitella, Petramarcia … .

'Fancy that!' he exclaimed aloud, delighted his memory had retrieved his old theory of feelings as places.

The other gave him a sharp look, actually seemed to take offence: 'Think what you will,' he said, 'but I must tell you what is current opinion, otherwise I would not be acting like a friend.'

'Go on, tell me,' he encouraged him affably, for he still couldn't help feeling joyful.

'All right,' the other retorted, 'but for you what goes in one ear goes out the other.'

He answered with a laugh. Who knows the location of joy? he wondered, trying to retrace in his remotest memories that part of the landscape which contained it. Perhaps, he said to himself, it was not always a locality, occasionally it was something more accidental: for example, that bush they draped with a tablecloth one evening in June so it could dry.

In the meantime his interlocutor's pronouncements were becoming more and more sententious: *'Tertium non datur'* he was saying and resorted to citing proverbs, each time tugging his sleeve or slapping his arm or simply pushing his hand away to prevent him from drinking whenever he reached for the bottle. 'Once on shore we pray no more.' 'When the cat's away the mice play,' 'Who laughs last laughs longest,' he finally wound up, emphatically removing the bottle to the far edge of the table.

He nodded. 'Who salts the soup doesn't somersault through the window!' he declared in turn. And while the other asked for some light on this last pronouncement, he managed to take the bottle, poured himself a drink and began in turn a list of all the proverbs he knew and then of rhyming phrases with a proverbial ring. It's up to me to say something too, he thought. It would not be civil to remain totally silent.

On the other hand, whether he spoke or not, the simple fact of being in the company of this old man seemed increasingly odd to him. 'How does he come into it?' he wondered. And the question irresistibly extended to others: the waiter, the bartender and the cook who by turn appeared or disappeared according to some inscrutable impulse like beasts who for no apparent reason stick their noses outside their burrows to explore. Ah, the immense stupidity of that exploration! What has the world to say to them and what could they possibly have to say to the world? What is the significance of these characters? he wondered. What is the significance of the characters in my life? Those I hit, others I only threaten to hit and those I reassure, promise not to lay a finger on, such as this old man, and his secretary, and the porter to whom he had said that very morning: 'No need to keep your back to the wall every time you see me.' They appear and disappear: it is all a matter of peeping out of the burrow and then popping back into the shadows, perhaps forever. In general this behaviour is typical of the entire animal world. So how can significance be attributed to a dog or a cat or a man or a whore? A tree is totally different! he told himself, gratefully glancing through the window.

He resumed his observation of the old man and it suddenly struck him that he had eyes like those of a dog that he had seen as a boy. He had pulled it to his chest so he could blow on its muzzle. The dog's eyes were pulled wide open by the skin stretched tight on either side of its ears which he had grabbed to hold it still, and those round reddened eyes even as they stared back at him were already fleeing to thoughts of its lair.

And where were the sly eyes of the old man fleeing, while they stayed fixed on him?

He felt his head spin. What's happening! he said to himself. Drunk already? Although he couldn't believe it, his head continued to spin.

Perhaps I'm not tipsy, he told himself. Not yet. It is an objective fact that the world spins and every so often you feel it. You realise that the present has shifted by a few degrees with respect to the past or that all at once the present has overwhelmed everything that ever was, in just the space of a minute, even a single second.

'Don't let it bother you!' he said, flashing the other a broad grin.

'Why should I let it bother me?' the old man exclaimed. 'Why should I be bothered when you laugh? It seems to me,' he said, 'that you're the one who should look in a mirror! Take a look in the mirror next time you laugh,' he suggested rudely.

He promised he would take the next opportunity to do just that and they both fell silent, as if by common consent.

After all, he thought, somewhat put out, he's the one who should be doing the talking. It's his investigation. But as the minutes went by in silence, the feeling of being put out faded little by little and his spirit became imbued with a sort of inertia. Something was certainly overwhelming without managing to be anything more real than the air imperceptibly darkening.

Night is coming, that's all! he decided. And he considered how many times this slow failing of the light had been the dominant note of his life.

'If I could only manage to sleep,' he confided to the old man, 'I'd be more content. Do you sleep?' he asked.

'It's the wine that won't let you sleep,' the other replied. 'When I drink the way I have with you this evening, I can't sleep either.'

What is important in life besides sleep? he wondered and the question saddened him. It would be nice if there were something, he told himself. Sleep is not much, really not very much at all. He tried to think of other things besides sleep, probably pleasant, at least for some people: wine, which for him had never been truly pleasurable, whores, with whom he was often content, work ...

'Some people love their work,' he declared.

The other shrugged and he himself laughed. Certainly the idea of loving work was absurd and yet, he admitted, he liked his office: at least the place itself. Where else would he have gone? Why leave the house in the morning? Certainly he could go around town hitting more people, many more people; establish a certain frequency and keep to it: clout someone every ten minutes for instance. Or invent rules for grading the hits, awarding more or less points.

'And your work?' he asked.

The other looked at him silently for a moment or two: 'It goes on,' he finally declared and lapsed into silence again.

Perhaps he wants to say something to me in private: recommend somebody for a study grant or some other favour, he thought. Perhaps I should encourage him: 'What do you think of our awards for the arts?' he asked.

The fellow seemed taken aback at first, but then, tapping his forehead to indicate sudden illumination, he broke into a laugh: 'That one to the nephew of the grand vizier?' he asked.

'What's that got to do with it?' he retorted, 'That was last year and there is nothing funny about it. Art with a capital A, my friend. Haven't you ever heard of spontaneous art? There are, it appears, some innocents who paint, and innocence aside, I have been told of an idiot who is nonetheless a pianist of international renown. Art is made with the heart, and you could say with the balls, never with the head: that is only good for making money.'

'Balls!' the fellow replied. 'Now we know you reckon it was a stitch-up.'

'You think so?' he asked coldly.

'Go on!' the other said conciliatingly. 'I know you had no option. And then,' he added, 'what is this renewable award contract? One of the many annuities that go to all and sundry today?'

He gave a shrug: 'Water under the bridge.'

The old man continued to snigger: 'Oh, yes! Today it's enough to be in the pockets of any doorman to get an arts handout. But that wouldn't interest a vizier, certainly not the money. He would want the intellectual consecration of his nephew: insane, of course, but an artist. In other words, he wanted the ritual and he got it.'

'Forgive me,' he resumed and then spent a full minute guffawing all by himself, despite being eyed with feigned disbelief. 'It is not the lunatic as such who amuses me, even though he was spattering drool all over the place, it's the solemnity of it all. I can practically see it: you're handing him the piece of paper (or was it a parchment?) while his eyes are bursting out of his head fastened on your secretary's big bum: 'Fuck, fuck!' he shouts through the slobber as he goes for her, trying to pull out his prick. But they had sewn up his pants, they had!'

'All right,' he conceded, 'He's not much of an artist, he's an idiot. So what! Art today, to paraphrase Dante, has such big arms it embraces all who turn towards it. But what does this have to do with your investigation?'

'Nothing at all,' the other replied. 'I just said it for a laugh. And then I'm glad to see you obey the orders of your superiors like everyone else. It's a point in your favour, as they say: most reassuring. Next to that, who cares if one more good-for-nothing gets slapped around?'

'Do you like this wine?' he asked, to change the subject. Then noticing that the bottle was almost empty he shouted irritably: 'Wine! Wine!' while gesturing wildly to the waiter. He didn't like wine, he explained, but it induced a feeling of calm, like a shady corner in a garden, with round clouds above the treetops: 'Poplars or beeches,' he said. 'Pines wouldn't suit, not in this case'

'But what about your health?' the other objected.

He nodded gravely and they began to discuss ailments such as cirrhosis and delirium tremens. At a certain point he suggested almost affectionately it might be advisable for the old man to get a check-up. 'When one reaches a certain age,' he said, 'it is important to find out what still works and what is definitely worn out, otherwise when the time comes how will one distinguish between a drunken stupor and a coma?'

And since the other looked dumbfounded he went on to explain that death does not come with trumpets and drums, announcing: 'I am death'. It is a moment like any other, which all at once overwhelms all past moments; but the fact of being the last does not give it the right to special fanfare. 'You think you are doing something or other, like drinking, for example,' he said, 'and perhaps death and this moment of drinking are as similar as two drops of water!'

'Bugger that!' the other broke in, vigorously slapping his open palm against his extended right arm.

For some time they both laughed heartily and as the laughter died away he felt a nostalgia for the country, and for healthy country habits; for wine and peasant jokes, and for living in the country as well, in a house among trees with a vegetable garden: not in his family house, though, which he still possessed and which had always seemed far too large and pompous to him, but in another. Wherever it might be, this unknown house was certainly now wrapped in late autumn fog, lamenting its state of abandonment with moaning pipes, creaking beams and mice scampering in the attic. 'Poor house!' he half-whispered. Through the window onto the deserted street a branch of the dark motionless tree seemed to be listening.

'Every once in a while,' he confided to the other, who for the moment had stopped talking and drinking and was now studying him closely, 'every once in a while, as I was saying, I think I would like to buy a house in the country.'

'Abroad!' the other advised him. 'Always buy property abroad. One fine day if you have to make a run for it, at least you have a place to go.'

He shook his head: It was not a practical idea, he explained, it was a recurring image. Often he saw this house in a very general way, as if the word house were illustrated. 'It must be some sort of symbol,' he said. Like the wine which he didn't enjoy and yet which suggested a certain calm to him.

'Aha!' the other exclaimed.

'It could also be,' he went on, 'that when a person's ideas are muddled, as often happens with drink, he attaches them to the first words that come to mind, so that an identification occurs: the muddled ideas take on the significance of those very words.'

The other looked at him: 'Explain something to me,' he said. 'Applying your theory, isn't it also possible that beating people up signifies your muddled ideas?'

'Well,' he said, 'to a certain extent it may be possible, but only to a certain extent. Actually,' he continued, 'a beating is purely practical: that is, I hit people because I am able to hit them. Therefore hitting signifies power; actually, in my case is power, the manner in which I personally exercise it.'

The other nodded contritely: 'I understand,' he said.

'And then,' he went on, 'a beating can signify various other things according to the circumstances.'

The waiter came towards them from the back of the room. He was of medium height, middle-aged, impeccably dressed in black with a white shirt. As he passed a few feet away the man shot him a quick glance of understanding, but open and frank, without a hint of complicity. Then he turned to the next table and started to adjust the tablecloth, straightening its folds.

Now the silence was so acute that the waiter's hand could be heard smoothing the cloth.

Everything appeared as orderly as it was inconsequential, or perhaps more accurately everything seemed to be progressing in orderly fashion, with good grace even, towards nightfall and meaninglessness. Anyhow, there would be an evening like this tomorrow and likewise the day after tomorrow and all the months to come, repetition replacing all significance.

'Shall we meet here tomorrow evening?' he asked.

The other made an evasive gesture: 'I must say that it's very kind of you to invite me. But if I may be permitted an expression of sincerity, you never fail to astound me. Another evening? Does time mean nothing to you?'

'As you wish' he said.

Both shook their heads. The light had so weakened that the place could now definitely be called dark, but so peaceful that he felt no need to ask them to turn on the lights in the room.

'It's dark and they haven't turned on the lights,' the old man complained after a few moments.

'What's the hurry?' he asked. 'After all,' he explained, 'these are the dead hours for business. Too early for the restaurant, too late for the bar.'

'Dead hours?' the old man said, emptying the last of the bottle into his own glass. 'They are for me too.'

He nodded, but suddenly to him these hours seemed to be not so much dead as moribund: or rather all the hours and days and years in their inertia revolved like a merry-go-round, whose circular significance seemed to be death. *Mal te perdoneran a ti las horas/ las horas que limando estan los dias/ los dias que royendo estan los años ...*

'Stop fussing with those tablecloths,' he said to the waiter, who was now attending to another table. He nodded and moved away silently.

'Well,' said the old man, straightening up against the back of his chair, 'we've seen in the evening.'

'What else were you wanting to know about the beatings?' he queried.

'Me?' the man queried in his turn. 'Oh, yes! They have a special significance, you were saying.' He scratched his hands nervously. 'Give me an example.'

'For example,' he replied, 'I certainly wouldn't hit the Minister of the Interior ...'

'Of course not!' the other chuckled. 'That would be unthinkable.'

'All right,' he said, 'but now consider some poor fellow walking along all by himself in worn-out shoes, smelly and exhausted. He is trudging along thinking about his wife, who is also tired and also smelly, and he is thinking about their sick and smelly children, and the hovel in which they live without water, except when it rains, and which is likewise always smelly: and while he thinks about all this and other things even worse, suddenly I come up and land him two clouts over the ears. Now do you understand?'

'Oh,' the other said. 'What am I supposed to understand?'

'How edifying it is: it could be called a moral gesture,' he protested. 'At least I imagine that boxing his ears should transform that familiar litany of woes to which we all get accustomed into an instantaneous and illuminating festival of calamities.'

'And so?' the other asked, ever more baffled.

'And so, then it is possible, I say only possible, that the man will put cyanide in the water supply or pour petrol into the cellars of the Grand Hotel, or some other such thing. Don't you see?' he asked.

'All right,' the other admitted. 'It is just possible he might do it, but what would you get out of it?'

'Ah,' he said, shaking his head ruefully. 'Myopic souls don't see significance, even when it is right in front of their noses. Don't you understand? This is its obvious sense: the glory of its explicit sense, I would be so bold as to say: that in one fell swoop it transforms the calamity of being alive into a flaming triumph of fury.'

The other squirmed in his chair, plainly vexed.

'And what about you? That fellow tosses in some cyanide. But you! You, I say. If anything he is the one who feels triumph of fury or whatever you called it. But I wonder what it does for you?'

'What do you mean, what does it do for me?' he protested. 'I witness this transformation. Aside from my modest contribution, in the sense of having set this event in motion with a simple clout, what counts when it is a matter of significance is not the action but the seeing and the understanding. And who would be in a better position to see and understand than I am?'

The other bent his head and flung out his arms in exasperation, then turned on the edge of his chair pointedly staring out of the window.

'So,' he eventually resumed, 'how should I report on these beatings of yours?'

'Has my proposition about the glory of significance escaped you?' he asked.

'In part,' the other admitted, 'probably most of it. The best I think I could say is that you are hunting for glory.'

'Well,' he approved, 'it's your report. You'll find that no matter what you say, they'll be happy.'

The other nodded and said nothing, still turned aside gazing out of the window.

Perhaps I exaggerated with this story of glory, he thought. 'The truth is,' he said aloud, 'that I am not content either. Yet look at me. Why should I not be content? Because of this lantern jaw? Well, some people with hunchbacks are content, not to mention that with all the advances in surgical techniques, perhaps soon it will be possible to cut off a lantern jaw and not cut off a hump. Of course I can't sleep. But perhaps I don't sleep for the very reason that I am not content, rather than, as I usually believe, I am not content because of lack of sleep. The discontent, therefore, does not originate with me, but from outside, from the world, let's say.'

'Don't you like the world?' asked the old man. 'What is it you don't like? Winter? Summer? Society?'

'Who mentioned society?' he interrupted. 'Everyone gets something out of it. Isn't this society?'

'And those who get hit, what do they get out of it?'

'Ah!' he laughed. 'I suspected you were a populist. If they get hit it means they are alive. Who would hit a dead man? Isn't being left alive what they get out of it?'

The other did not reply; but folded his arms obstinately across his chest.

Maybe, he thought to himself, we're both of us drunk. And after saying this, he too sat silently looking straight ahead into the empty room, with tables, tablecloths and waiter almost submerged in the gathering darkness. A few minutes of excessive, almost theatrical calm went by. When he turned to look at his neighbour he saw only his body mass: a shadow almost indistinguishable even against the light, quietly swaying, head drooping on his chest. So then he stretched across the table to strike him on the shoulder:

'Don't meditate!' he exhorted him.

In the meantime, the table at the other end of the room had been taken by a middle-aged woman with bright pink lipstick and pale opaque skin, possibly due to too much powder, so far as he could tell at a distance of about ten yards. She had clear eyes in dark sockets.

'What a sad whore!' he said. 'Look at her!'

The other shrugged his shoulders, but after some prodding turned his head: 'How ridiculous!' he said. 'Why sad?' According to him she was neither sad nor cheerful, just neutral. 'The world,' he proclaimed, 'doesn't give a damn: the world is neutral.' So they talked about the neutrality of the world and of whores.

Meanwhile they had each drunk two glasses from a new bottle, and he thought it was time for a third. The bottle stood on the table, but the other man guarded it with the tips of his fingers, barely touching it, and discouraging any approaches with a stern expression.

The light had become not only faint but grey and the consequent feeble local colour made the sad whore in her distant corner, the bottle, and the bough outside the window all seem like participants in the same fate, furled banners, emblems of the close of day.

Seen from this point of view, the neutrality of the world weighed heavily on his eyelids: darkness now blurred the outlines of objects inside the cafe, and outside the evening pallor with its submerged vistas looked more than ever like a setting for a collective funeral. 'How many dead?' a loud-speaker enquired with bureaucratic calm and like everyone else he too enumerated his own dead: 'Let's see,' he said, uncertain, 'my mother, for a start.'

'And then?' the voice insisted.

'My mother, I said,' he repeated.

Then he remembered better: 'Ah, yes,' he said. 'My father is also dead.'

At this point, compelling himself to remember more, everything seemed to go dark and became indecipherable. Not only H and Z were hard to tell apart, but sometimes even the As and Ns. 'I have passed the point' he thought. Sometimes in fact his imagination would slip into a condition which might more appropriately be called sleep or near-sleep.

'You know,' he said, turning to the other, 'I almost fell asleep?'

'Well, look at that!' the other replied, not even looking. Silence fell again so heavily that he imagined it would take a great exertion to lift. And then? he asked himself. There was something desperately repetitive in the situation: once overcome, the moment would reassert itself, always requiring yet another great exertion and yet another and still more, until the moment he surrendered once and for all. To what? he thought. To sleep? And why not? Wasn't sleep what he needed?

He shook his head dejectedly. Then just to do something leaned across the table again to poke his companion, who was silently studying the inside of his empty glass.

'It seems to be my destiny!' he said. 'I never manage to get a good sleep.'

The other nodded with the ready commiseration of a drunk. 'Destiny, bloody destiny!' And he concluded this declaration with a sigh, grabbing a fresh bottle which had evidently arrived at the table when he wasn't paying attention, and poured him a generous glassful with steady hand. 'The mill doesn't grind without water!' the other announced, while his fingertips pushed the over-full glass towards him with inviting nudges.

'Those who piss in the wind piss backwards!' he himself added, lowering his lips to the rim of the glass. The white wine, dry and cold, tasted slightly of soap, and when he studied the colour, it looked to him more pale grey than golden.

Why sad? he pondered, suddenly thinking about the whore. Neutral really wasn't the right word: serious would be better. Fixed as she was in her corner in a posture that was apparently habitual, he imagined a soul rendered half-anxious and half-drowsy, accustomed to whiling away the late afternoon sitting in a cafe, awaiting, as if from time immemorial, a night of trekking between bidet, wash basin and latrine: a night, so to speak, with arse in hand, uncomfortable certainly, but in its own way almost stoically austere.

He raised his arm above his head and tried to catch her eye, wiggling his fingers and keeping up a continuous signal. For some time the woman ignored his signal. Then she looked at him and looked again at ever-shorter intervals until her face, without losing its composure, assumed an insulting smirk. The insult of the smirk, in the overall severity of her face, gave her the appearance of a tragic queen, almost as though great and solemn words were about to issue from the rigid immobility of the mouth in her mask.

In the meantime, summoned by the signal that he still held high, the waiter had returned to their table and stood looking at him questioningly.

'What do you want?' he snapped, lowering his arm. But since the man assumed a conciliatory expression, to placate him he explained that his gesture had been directed 'at the lady'.

'I'm going to propose a toast,' he said, getting to his feet. Wrenching the bottle from his companion's grasp and pouring himself half a glass, he started to declaim more than sing: '*Vivan le femmine, viva il buon vino, gloria e sostegno di umanità.*'

'You massacred every note!' the other cried, slapping his knee. The waiter smiled, shaking his head as if to recommend forbearance. The other in the meantime whined out something he presumably supposed was the right tune.

Glory and pillar of humanity, he repeated to himself inwardly and imagined this glory steadily advancing out of the darkness into the light with the tread of an army of pale-faced women, but powerful and huge as warrior-mothers. If only it were true! he thought. He would have raced ahead to denounce all offences and abuses for everything to be set right, and so with justice restored, a bright and caressing sun would once more shine down upon, as the poet wrote, 'a human and progressive destiny'.

He smiled at this imagined light and glory, meanwhile straining his eyes to see to the far end of the room and the woman at her table near the entrance who was ever more difficult to discern, being almost enveloped in the advancing dusk; or rather herself become part of the dusk and the cold and the neutrality of a November verging on December, just as the dusk verged on night. But then at a certain point this nocturnal champion of womankind, in her own way both pale and powerful and yet more perversely stern than glorious, very deliberately turned to him and stuck out a huge tongue, whiter even than her face, and wagged it around. Almost as if her tongue were a magic wand, suddenly the dark obliterated every trace of that inward light, every extravagant dream of glory.

Every object, indistinct in the gloom, at once seemed to appropriate its own measure of darkness. He felt he was emanating obscurity himself. Everything was at the same time conventional and final, as it generally is in the provinces. Outside the cafe too, he imagined the relentless all-levelling dusk permeating everything, not this actual November dusk which intervened in a year of his life, but the astronomical dusk falling in the existence of the world. Slowly but surely, as this ultimate dusk descended, the iridescent caprices of present imagination became ever more laboured and difficult, leaving to the objects scattered around nothing but their most summary outlines, as though stranded: bottles, faces, harsh transparencies of glass, the glint of metal or mirror.

In her corner meanwhile, the whore who was now weary from exercising her tongue so vigorously turned her face and gazed at the window, not by chance or for amusement but almost by virtue of an impulse as pre-ordained as the motion of sunflowers. Essentially everything looked prepared. The great scheme of things held sway, as well as the sense of suffocation that purportedly goes with the scheme. No place more than the provinces acquiesces more easily to cosmic regularity, to the alternation of seasons, the litany of months, the succession of afternoons, evenings and nights, right down to the almost imperceptible but unstoppable passing of minutes and almost even of seconds.

And then? he asked himself.

'And then?' he asked in a loud voice.

The waiter leaning on the bar whispering with the bartender turned to look at him. The coffee machine released a whitish cloud of steam with a whistle that seemed almost polite; his companion suddenly sat up straight in his chair: 'Without eating!' he said, 'We have drunk three bottles without eating.'

'Four' he corrected.

'Four' the man admitted, meticulously scratching the back of one hand and then the other.

Things were at this point when suddenly all the lights came on. From every socket holder and light fixture, from every direct or indirect source, a sea of light flooded the room. Now, and there was no denying it, the circumspect oppression of a provincial nether world was replaced by the exuberance of an operatic ballroom scene, with goblets gleaming, though lamentably empty.

'And now how about a brandy?' he said.

'What?' the other retorted' 'are we out of our minds?'

'Your talk about the neutrality of the world,' he said, 'interests me greatly. What were you saying?'

The old man gave a shrug. 'The world doesn't give a damn,' he said. 'It goes its own way!'

From a distance he saw the world going its own way with exasperating slowness. Lights would be coming on in other cafes; elsewhere, unhurriedly, almost with repugnance, an alley, a street, a square, was laboriously settling down for the night with a show of lights in the windows on facades long blackened with shadows. And what of the villages and towns nearby? And those further away situated on different longitudes with different time zones?

On the other hand inside the bright cafe events were occurring with a rapidity that seemed comparatively festive. For example: another woman had entered, going up to the bar at first but now seated next to the sad whore: a tall attractive young woman whose hand grasped a big glass full of green liquid, showing up her white metallic nail varnish. The old man who had been observing him for some minutes with a sort of torpid stupor now bent to look for something in the pocket of his coat on the chair nearby. He rummaged without moving his head, keeping his eyes on the window. Beyond the window to the left of him everything was decidedly black, save for a faint glow in the sky above the line of rooftops: light no longer but a white like white lead, cracked and tarnished.

At this point a woman of average height with her hair drawn back in a bun and a coat with vertical green and white stripes, after hesitating a good minute holding the door ajar, entered the place, accompanied by a rush of cold air from the street.

'The slag patrol has called a meeting!' his colleague commented, turning to watch her. He laughed to seem polite and the other man laughed in return and so alternately each responded to the other, laughing in each other's face.

On account of these events or the apparently unusual pace of their sequence, everything seemed to be undergoing a metamorphosis. And yet, on reflection, rather than a transformation it seemed to him that people and things were preparing for transfer, proceeding now by common accord towards some new orbit. His table companion, who by this time was the only one laughing, the three women, silent and composed at their tables, the waiter leaning on the bar with an abandon apparently untouched by any sort of preoccupation, seemed intent only on distancing themselves from the world, motivated by other interests which were not necessarily more lofty. Tomorrow would be another day and before that another night would come, it seemed they were saying. So, farewell. It is destiny to part company, leaving each to his own supper, to his lovers and above all to his own sleep. Only he would be left alone and sleepless, despite foolishly closing his eyes from time to time …

'So they've dropped you, haven't they?' his mother asked with her implacable air of peevishness.

He would have liked to convince her, certainly not that he had not been dropped, which seemed incontrovertible, but to convince her of something more general: so general, in fact, that everything would change for the better if he could succeed in convincing her. Joy would be established in the house in place of frowns, and kindness in place of spite. In his imagination, at least, he knew he was an expert in the art of disputation and therefore did not despair that some day or other she would be convinced. But suddenly his mother was dead. 'She is dead!' they had informed him and had taken him to see her. If only he had known her death was imminent just a day, even an hour ahead of time, he told himself, he surely would have succeeded in convincing her, but she died so suddenly he hadn't even had the chance to try, and now his arts of persuasion, honed in the course of long sleepless nights, seemed to him futile delirium.

'It's your jaw!' the other mumbled. 'The women are talking about your lantern jaw.'

He shrugged nonchalantly: 'Everyone talks about it,' he said. 'They've always talked about it.'

At the back of the room the sad whore sneezed. The old man returned his coat to the back of the chair and now held a dirty handkerchief in his hand. The waiter leaning against the bar stared at the glass door and beyond, presumably at the street which was now also lit up and looked yellowish on the other side of the glass, deserted, nocturnal.

So much concentration, he thought, so much seriousness! And possibly all they're thinking about is my jaw. The last to arrive in fact was staring straight at him: 'Hey, look at that lantern jaw!' he sensed those eyes of hers were saying. All the same, this prattle in the whore's eyes remained inside her head, unspoken: that is, it possessed the silent dignity of thought. And suddenly that coy repressed thought seemed so pregnant with mystery as to equal, at least in melancholy, the mysteries of the universe, the various forms of ignorance that hold dominion over men and contain their destiny. He smiled at her. 'What can we do about it?' he thought in reply. And she seemed to agree and lowered her eyes.

'If it were me,' his table companion said under his breath as though talking to himself, 'I'd give her a good wallop.'

'If you must know,' he informed the fellow, 'I never wallop anyone, but only cuff them gently with the palm of the hand from the base of the neck upwards. And this is hard to manage when women have long hair.'

'Oh, that's a good one! Never wallop anyone?' He was astounded. 'Then, what's everyone talking about?'

'Clips and cuffs,' he insisted. 'People are poorly informed. Perhaps at the beginning,' he explained, 'a few wallops might have even escaped me, but the human face possesses lips, a nose, eyes, all with mucous membranes that secrete fluids, without mentioning blood that flows readily: such dirtiness in other words is unhygienic for the hands. But hair, even dirty hair, I find less disgusting'

'Well, well,' the other said. 'If that's how it is, it's good to know. So it's enough not to turn one's back on you.'

'It's usually enough!' he admitted. But to put an end to the discussion he added that in difficult cases sometimes he circled his victim, until he had him confused, and got the chance to get in a whack. In any case, he concluded, it was nothing to get worked up about: often it was just fun and games and then, not least for humanitarian reasons, his actions could be called smacks rather than whacks.

'I see!' the old man exclaimed. 'Let's just say that you are a big joker.'

He put a finger to his lips: 'That's not true! And don't spread it around,' he cautioned. 'I wouldn't want people to treat me with too much familiarity. It is better to keep one's distance always, don't you agree?'

'Of course, of course!' the other assured him. 'And what about women? Doesn't it amuse you to give whores a few smacks?'

'Amuse me?' he asked. 'I never thought about it. But what would anyone find amusing in that? If anything,' he explained, 'there was actually a didactic intent at times.'

'Of course,' the other admitted, 'it is impossible to be always drinking, eating and screwing whores; it's good to fit in a little bit of a lesson. Yes, if I were you, every once in a while I'd give a whore a little smack myself. Right on her bum, eh?'

He smiled thinly and the man stopped talking. In his silence every once in a while the other pushed out his lips in a sort of perplexed pout. 'Ah, well!' he exclaimed. He appeared to be both irritated and sad, but eventually the sadness clearly prevailed. 'What could I have said to make him so sad?' he wondered, feeling sorry for him.

'Your investigation?' he finally asked. 'How is it going? Have you found out what you wanted to find out?'

The old man looked at him, scratching his hands: 'You are rich,' he said with a smile. 'You certainly don't need to do anything for money.'

'What's that have to do with it?' he asked. 'Apart from anything else,' he went on, 'it's not true. It could be said that I am well off, with an inheritance that might have been considered a fortune in a small town some years back: nothing like the new international riches, dazzling financial empires that have earned our politicians world-wide fame. My wealth is merely local.'

The other nodded repeatedly, still scratching his hands.

The old man's expression was benign and considerate, and seemed to resemble some other kindness in his distant past. 'What does it resemble?' he asked himself; but although the similarity was undeniable he could not pin it down. This time, however, instead of letting himself be oppressed by an unfathomable similarity, he sharpened his gaze towards his most distant memory: he saw his mother again, seated under the pergola with her eyes fixed on the line of trees at the edge of the woods with her usual frown of irritation. They say that she is rich, he had thought then, and her gaze seemed to him a sort of inspection of those riches. How many things those silent serious eyes had seen; unknown cities, mountains, plane trees along summer avenues, foyers of theatres and grand hotels. Her life had been a world and yet she was never content. But since it was a summer evening, in the moments which became cooler as the last rays of sun filtered through the pergola leaves makiing them shimmer in the freshening breeze, it had seemed to him that the rustling play of light and shade was gently urging her to be resigned, that luminous wavering at the margins of her dark thoughts could coax her into imagining a peaceful time without too many regrets. If he could have gone over to her then and talked to her with all the wisdom he already felt capable of deploying, holding his breath as though on tiptoe on the very brink of words, then perhaps his entire self, including his lantern jaw, might have been admitted to the periphery of her world. Almost unawares he had drawn close to her and touched her shoulder with his hand. 'Now what do you want?' she had turned on him. 'Why are you always such a nuisance?'

'But look, look at her now!' the old man burst out, 'They really do have it in for you. Do you see the signs they're making?'

In fact the stern whore who also looked the oldest and most authoritative of the three, staring straight at him, motioned with one hand now to her chin, now to her belly.

'So what are they saying?' the other asked.

He laughed and in reply mimicked a blow.

'That's right,' the old man approved, shouting enthusiastically. 'Give those foul whores a good trouncing!'

The waiter drew himself away from the bar and moved towards them.

'Be careful!' he whispered, leaning over them as if to tidy the table. 'Watch out for the old one's handbag, not the black one, the other long one with the embroidery. She keeps a brick sewn into the bottom of it.'

They thanked him.

When the waiter had gone, the other said, 'We could have them arrested and roughed up. But there wouldn't be any fun in that,' he sighed several times. 'You know what?' he finally concluded. 'I've had enough of this lousy place. If you don't mind, I think I'll make myself scarce.'

He approved: 'Go ahead!' he said.

The old man stood up and went to speak privately with the

waiter at a corner of the bar; the bartender was summoned as well, and after a short discussion he returned to the table.

'I've paid my share,' he reported. 'It's expensive here!'

'That wasn't necessary!' he said. 'Didn't I invite you?'

The other spread his arms and smiled as if to apologise for himself.

'Run along then!' he said, dismissing him with a nod of the head. 'Don't be late.'

The other turned, reached the glass door and vanished into the yellowish gloom of the street without a word.

And I only wanted to be civil, he said to himself, thinking back on the contemptible speed of the old man's departure into the shadows. Looking around, he noticed that the two younger whores had also left. Only the sad whore remained firm in her place, looking at him as severely as before. Almost without being aware of it, he repeated the old man's gesture, opened his arms and shrugged his shoulders as though to excuse himself and unexpectedly, unbelievably, the old whore responded with a smile.

# THE FIRST WHORE AND THE DEMON

It was so peaceful there or at least inert that he could have almost fallen asleep; but it did not seem quite the place for a decent sleep. Instead he allowed whims and stray thoughts to come at random to keep him company, while he sat quietly in a corner of the room.

It was cold and wet out in the street, which was a dead-end alley, and now inside he mentally retraced the route he had taken between successive cloudbursts in order to reach this place, which after all was just a run-down old brothel. He had heard something about a revival in business and that had been enough to start him crossing town. After all, what else was there to do at seven in the evening?

From outside, the house looked grim, almost hostile: the heavy iron gratings over the ground floor windows were adorned with plain rosettes of an almost military sobriety. The rusticated facade built of huge stone blocks, with projecting arches, tympanum and cornice, was so imposing in that narrow alley that it appeared menacing even in broad daylight, as he recalled.

The interior or rather the large room he found himself in now was divided into a central square area under a skylight about thirty feet across, with a sort of corridor or ambulatory on three of its sides: a strip about two yards wide with a lower ceiling than the central square and partitioned from it by comparatively slender columns that were undecorated, even squalid, faced with that type of slimy white marble once used in urinals.

The fourth side had four windows running from just above head height almost to the ceiling, draped with heavy curtains of some vague dark colour. Four huge radiators were positioned below each window. He presumed that these tall windows looked out on the alley. Apart from the entrance door, other doors led into other rooms. He had seen into two of them while crossing to the sofa, but from his present position they were now concealed by the columns. The walls and ceiling were a vague grey, with darker or lighter patches according to the degree of light and incorporated dirt. The sofas, all similar to the one on which he was sitting, some longer, some slightly shorter, were rectangular and heavy, with high-backed walnut frames. Covered in fake leather varying in colour from rosy red to brown, they were lined up almost touching each other along two of the walls. Against the wall facing him, beyond the columns, was a long table covered with a white cloth reaching to the floor and cluttered with big cardboard boxes and other smaller ones.

Even after detailed examination, there was something he found hard to explain about the place: curious acoustics, for a start. Although the building was for the most part silent, the rare sounds that occasionally reached his ears seemed to come from somewhere not so much distant as utterly separate and diverse: soft thuds or dry miaowings of cats or squeaking hinges which seemed to bear no relation to each other, so that the world of sounds appeared to operate according to a different logic from the world of silence, and both forms of logic were foreign to his normal mode of thinking. 'Effect of the wind!' he said to steady his nerves; but his explanation or perception of the sounds was, he felt, spurious: a perception without understanding, anxiously aware of its own failure to understand.

'I don't understand!' he admitted with growing agitation. Perhaps, on reflection, it was not the sounds that were incomprehensible (in fact as he listened more keenly he now felt with near certainty that he had correctly interpreted every squeak and creak as a product of the wind), it was the lights. Not that there was a shortage, in fact there were more than enough, but they were positioned on the ambulatory ceiling in a way that created more confusion than clarity. There was ample light, but light and objects looked disconnected. Perhaps, he thought, the lighting is too objective, too exact. Consequently, rather than casting shadows because of the light, objects seemed to possess their own shadows and, passing from consequence to consequence, rather than having a set position or purpose in a place, they appeared to take place, almost as if the space each item occupied and their ways of intercepting the light were not transitory but a permanent property, intrinsic to being box, chair, sofa. Seen in this way, the world of things also seemed to reassert its right to immobility: a duration of its own in its own time, independent of the circumstances. 'Tombstones,' he whispered. 'Amusing!' he concluded.

He tried to laugh softly under his breath, more to change the subject than because he was truly amused. I must admit I'm uncomfortable in this brothel, he thought. Certainly it was more like an ex-brothel than a brothel: it lacked the fullness of the term in various ways. There were no prostitutes in sight, which could mean that the room was only used for storage now, or it might even be a dressmaker's workshop he had been shown into through some misunderstanding.

'It's that man with the lantern jaw!' the woman at the door had shouted to someone looking down from the top of the stairs. 'Shall I call the demon?'

'No! Certainly not!' a woman's voice had replied out of the darkness above. He had tried in vain to catch sight of her, and after a few imprecations, accompanied by a scrabbling of some animal's paws on the marble stairs, the beast evidently quietened down, and the same voice had added: 'Show him into the room. I will be there in a minute.'

'What breed is the demon?' he had asked the old woman who accompanied him.

'He's not a dog,' she had replied tartly. 'He is a dwarf.' He accepted the explanation without being wholly convinced, for the pawing on the stairs which he had heard distinctly for a few seconds sounded more like a big dog than a dwarf. And yet, he said to himself, I must admit that the sounds here are so odd they could easily be different from what they seem. He looked around, examining every corner with care, almost with apprehension.

A few yards from the sofa, through a gap where the curtains were loosely drawn, he could see the lower ledge of a window, placed so high that his own head would barely have touched it and yet he imagined that going up to it he would have been able to look up from below into the deep chasm of the sky framed by the houses in the alley and, given such a wind, might even have caught sight of bits of garbage spinning on high: paper or rags which, light and bright, could soar high enough to capture roving streaks of light fleeing the city.

Occasionally as a child he had heard people talk about the way garbage flies. Apparently whenever something monstrous occurred, such as for instance a magistrate's verdict that appeared excessively severe, trash took to the air. It flew to save certain people's faces, it was said; but someone observed that all these scraps of trash that were constantly flying about might one day think they were birds and begin to sing; whereupon someone else with good sense would cite notable examples of the silencing of song-birds, as in the case of the so-called government coffee, administered by funnel to over-talkative prisoners.*

Despite these allusions to the just and proper silence of the dead, this topic of conversation had always taken a jocular turn, and as a result he had come to picture all these bits of garbage as not precisely overjoyed but at least carefree; sombre only in the sense of nocturnal. So he had imagined a clear night and this great liberating flight in the starlight: convoys of paper and rags cruising aloft with lips prudently sealed; silent, in short, except for a nasal refrain, melodious and only mildly melancholy.

Who knows when the whores will arrive! he said to himself, and yet one promised to come! He shifted his weight on the sofa, and its springs creaked. The fake leather stuck to his hands, doubtless impregnated with many years of sweat or other body fluids; otherwise he would have gladly stretched out on it. Possibly, he repeated to himself, he'd been misinformed. Times had changed; there were no more brothels now, because prostitutes were everywhere. All you had to do was go up to anyone and ask: 'How much?' In other words, poetry was dead, killed off by commerce.

He shook his head in dismay and lay back. With his head now so low that he could clearly see the entire skylight looming over the central square and within its black panes brief faint flashes, as of distant lightning. A storm coming or perhaps going, he said to himself, or perhaps it's already raining. In fact a rustling

---

*Translator's note: At this time the Christian Democrats and the Mafia were working together to silence any opposition by the use of poisoned drinks and 'Government coffee'.

disturbed the silence every once in a while: the rustle of raindrops in a squall, water ripped from the rim of the storm cruising miles away in the depths of the night. Even if everything in the room was odd, there was peace or at least a certain comfort, and the echo, almost the shadow of what it once had been; and here, more plausibly than in any other place, he could think back to the brothel of old, see the ghosts of ancient whores again swathed in light: some slender, others with big stomachs and arses, but all of them appealing, at least for what he regarded as essential: although they may have sniggered openly at his jaw and made other coarse jokes, each made him feel welcome to rest his head in her lap, lantern jaw and all, in fact sometimes he even felt caressed and protected.

He indulged in a smile. Certainly, he admitted, he was a habitué of brothels. He used to show up at any time: especially in the dead hours, on rainy midweek afternoons, Wednesdays, Thursdays, when he was the only outsider and used to eat with the whores, rest with them, but above all he talked, listening to their stories and telling stories he contrived, without fear of contradiction or being called a liar and humiliated.

Sometimes they refused to open the door. 'It's time to restore discipline,' they used to say. But he'd make so much noise, shouting and banging on the door and finally resorting to big stones that eventually they were forced to yield. 'What's the big hurry,' the woman opening the door used to shout. 'Running to mamma, eh!'

'Out of my way!' he would say, pushing her aside. For these references to his mother distressed him, not least because in a remote corner of his mind, unsaid, actually unsayable, lurked the hope that by convincing the whores, he might also convince his mother. What lay behind this equivalence? he wondered now. And convince them of what? But, tentatively at least, he would begin to tell long fantastical stories in part spoken or sayable, in part silent, indecipherable to anyone, even himself.

He wanted to take her on a long journey, he would say to one or other of his favourites, and sometimes they discussed the route together, and made plans. There were some marvellous towns, claimed those who had travelled, and they would describe these places that they had seen or rather surmised from behind the brothel walls. Cities viewed from the side of silence:

nefarious and stony-hearted, yet ephemeral. Then one of them would push him away with sudden anger like a petulant lover. Which one? Who among all of them was this lover-whore about whom he still fantasised with so much regret?

Yes, he had to admit, his regret was total, pro indiviso, that all had vanished for ever and now he could only recall them in their essence, each a nebulous phantom of all: each the quintessential whore, and yet whoever this lover-whore might be, still today years later he continued to offer her words and pay her imagined compliments with a spontaneous ease born of ceaseless conversation, despite intervals which may have been long but were merely incidental.

And what would they talk about? Sometimes he seemed to hear their voices again with their own specific inflections almost as though they were present. But it was an awkward and unfulfilled present, as when one's memory is at fault, side-tracked by marginal considerations. It seemed to him their tales unfailingly contained sincere and heart-rending reminiscences of their far-off nameless towns, ruined towers and vast plains crushed beneath the eternal shadows of storm clouds. There were also tales of adversity and lovers alone and palely loitering in misty autumnal regions as though they were adventures of Lancelot of the Lake, errant in the land of Nod. Yet always something was omitted, something was missing. He tried to convince them of these omissions, not so much to force them to admit they were suppressing something (that would have been crass and carping), but to convince them that their silences contained something they failed to grasp. In short, the thing that he sought, he told himself inwardly smiling in self-commiseration, was to restore the omission, fill the vacuum and attain the whole: achieve the fulfilment and perfection, if only in words, of a perfect past. In terms of whores at least, for him fulfilment and what he called conviction were complementary.

He thought for a moment. Well, he decided. Let's just say a sort of fulfilment. Not fulfilment on the grand scale, just on the domestic level, one you can put out your hand and actually touch and say, even if with resignation: This is all!

Undoubtedly the expression 'fulfilment', taken in these narrow terms, could still imply the presence of something else beyond the walls of the brothel and its unvarying light. But whatever lay between one polar cap and the other could not but be incarnate now, embodied in the present, if it wished to exist. All existence in any one of the whores, even the yearning to exist, was gathered fully and instantaneously in the dark depths of her eyes, even when *nubila et inania captabant*.

What else?

Sometimes he would imagine renting an apartment in town and offering it free to the first of them to finish her term in a whorehouse and to want a bit of a rest before starting in another. So then he and the first whore would set off together to find this hypothetical retreat.

Of course there was nothing attractive about the town right outside the brothel walls. Most of the cracked and peeling houses in the narrow alley were other brothels or the humble dwellings of trouser or shirt-makers. The hum of sewing machines whirred through the stale air with relentless urgency to the exclusion of almost any other sound, so that a sense of haste predominated, evoking a general tedium. But other parts of town were quiet, at times virtually empty. In the public gardens by the sea, for instance, on certain winter afternoons not even a dog was about, or only glimpsed slinking by in a hurry, with ruffled pelt and tail between its legs even when there was no wind, scampering from one bush of pitosforum to another, or from one piss to the next, almost surreptitiously, scarcely daring to look round. For their own part they would mostly gaze out at the horizon, which on rainless days (but often in winter burdened by dense calm clouds) showed as a strip of light between the dark of the sea and the dark of the clouds, so still it did not even look like sky, but a geometric emanation of the difference between two darknesses.

Unfortunately houses with a view of the sea were the most expensive and very few had apartments for rent. So they would wander into more modest parts of town. Behind massive front doors, beyond entries and stairways of a certain pretension, empty corridors and rooms would greet the alien visitors with a sort of sullen expectancy. Groping onwards hesitantly they would stand and stare at the upholstered chairs, the wardrobes, the beds, assailed with misgiving as they contemplated the rent and the light from the narrow street seeping through drab windows and settling soundlessly over the furniture. Obviously other people had passed through these rooms and the drudgery of their unknown lives hung heavy in the air exactly as in his mother's room. She was dead and yet the difficulty or rather discontent of her life lingered on like a black phantom that could not decide whether to depart or to speak. 'Go on, make up your mind,' he would urge the whore. But she would shake her head sadly. 'Is there nothing else?' she would ask timidly. And even though they searched all over, they finally had to admit there was nothing else. 'This is all!' both would say, acknowledging that all for what it was.

He felt a hand on his shoulder and looked up. Leaning over him was a finely-drawn face haloed by hair suffused in a harsh white light. Overhead, the skylight was now lit with longer flashes of lightning, still soundless, but somewhere a sound of dripping more sonorous than the steady rustle of rain drummed the time.

'Ah!' he said, sitting up straight. 'Are you the first?' he asked, glancing about the room which was still deserted.

'The first what?' asked the woman, also straightening up.

'The first whore,' he said gruffly. 'Where are the others?'

She started to laugh softly (and most charmingly, he thought) 'I understand ,' she eventually said. 'You are still thinking of the old brothel from before, crammed with prostitutes. But it's not like that now!'

'Not like that?' he asked, puzzled.

'Not like that!' she insisted patiently. 'Don't you see?'

He got to his feet and began to make his apologies. He had been misinformed, he said. And in any case he would be going as soon as the rain died down. He pointed at the skylight: 'Is it leaking?' he asked. 'Do you hear that dripping?'

She shrugged: 'Everything needs fixing' she admitted.

'In any case, I'm pleased to meet you,' he said, abruptly extending a hand to her. 'And thanks for the hospitality.'

She took his hand, executing a sort of ballet curtsey.

'You were not so very mistaken,' she said, laying a hand on his shoulder. 'As for whores, we're whores,' she confessed lightly. 'Same as in your day, let's say, if not better. But there are not so many of us now: a little co-operative, five in all, and we don't call ourselves whores, or prostitutes or harlots.'

'Is that so?' he said, his curiosity aroused.

'Yes,' she said, leading him towards the door. 'We haven't yet chosen a name, but we would like something dignified, with cultural connotations. What do you reckon? Today culture is in fashion also because of tourism.'

By this time they had reached the door and he stopped. 'Perhaps!' he said. 'But right now it is pouring with rain and I don't even have an umbrella. I never carry one, damn it!'

She laughed her quiet laugh again: 'I am not showing you the door,' she said. 'We are dining upstairs and we'd like to invite you to join us. How silly of me not to say so at once!'

'Invite me to supper?' he exclaimed. 'In this weather?'

'What has the weather to do with it? I mean, where else would you go?' They argued for a little while, he offering to pay for dinner for everyone, and she refusing. By the time they were finally making their way to the stairs, they had broken the ice and were exchanging civilities.

'Now let's see,' he said, as they reached the first floor. 'What were you saying about cultural connotations?'

'A joke!' she laughed. 'And yet we could get a name like that printed on our visiting cards. Who would stop us?'

On the landing they went through the first door on the right into the dining room: a square room some fifteen feet across with a round table in the middle beneath a glass chandelier and in a corner by the window one of those little divans backed only at one end which were called Josephines or Paolinas in his family's house. There was other furniture as well: a few chairs in addition to those set round the table, and a sideboard with shelves. Plates and glasses gleamed on the tablecloth.

'Ah,' he approved. 'Very beautiful.'

His hostess lifted her eyes to him with a flash of gratitude. Her eyes were light, perhaps greenish, and her eyebrows thick and black, possibly a bit heavy; but the total effect made her gaze appear almost autonomous, or at least gave it priority over her other features. It was, in other words, one of those faces that are said to speak with the eyes.

'Have you finished examining me?' she asked. 'Am I to your taste?'

He assured her that she aroused his unconditional admiration and began to complement her for every aspect of her face and detail of her body. While he was praising her bare arms which emerged from a simple sleek grey dress, two young women came into the room.

'Here are my friends,' she said. They nodded their heads in greeting, but keeping to the other side of the table. They were about the same height as the first whore: one had red hair with a freckled rather square face and a stout body, wrapped in a green dress that left her heavy thighs half bare; the other was slender with a mass of black hair and a sleeveless dress in a dark colour, perhaps black, rich with intricate red embroidery. They both studied him without a word for a short time, and then sat down abruptly.

As he was taking his seat in turn, it seemed to him that the brunette made a face at the redhead. But the first whore, his hostess with the eloquent eyes, distracted him, telling him almost in his ear that her other friends didn't live with them.

'Although there is plenty of room,' she confided, 'they prefer their own families.'

'Of course' he agreed.

At that same moment the brunette burst out, almost at the top of her voice: 'Stop pulling! Don't touch me! And anyway why shouldn't I?' she went on, still almost shouting. 'They look at us as they please; they weigh us and fondle us with their eyes like hens at market. They make us go around on all fours, if they want, and I can't even look him in the face?'

'That's enough! Settle down!' the first whore interrupted her. 'She is so on edge' she said, turning to him apologetically.

'Ladies,' he said, 'if you are arguing about my lantern jaw, please don't. Feel free to look as much as you like. I am used to it. Actually, I could move to where the light is better, if you wish.'

The redhead broke into peals of laughter and the first whore echoed her, but her heart was not in it. Finally the brunette also raised her eyes to his face with a glance that was still suspicious if pacified. 'Yet,' she said, 'they say he lashes out to kill if anyone so much as mentions his jaw ...'

'That's not true,' he protested. 'I only hit people very gently, more out of affection than anything else, and never women.'

The brunette gave a scornful shrug: 'You try hitting me,' she promised, 'and I'll get the demon to rip off one of your balls.'

'That's enough nonsense!' the first whore intervened sternly.

The brunette shrugged again, this time as if to excuse herself, and gave the first whore a disarming smile.

'Who is the demon?' he asked.

At that moment the door opened and the concierge came into the room with a large soup tureen, declaring triumphantly: 'You are about to taste a wonderful soup!'

'Ah! fish, fish!,' the redhead exclaimed, 'my favourite food!'

'Don't guzzle,' the brunette warned her, 'or the bones will stick in your throat.'

The concierge placed the tureen on the table by the first whore and began to serve it herself so everyone could have some of each sort of fish. The bowls were passed from hand to hand.

'There are still a few shrimp left,' said the concierge.

'What about you two?' asked the redhead.

'You have them,' the woman responded, placing the tureen next to the redhead. 'Demon and I have already been served.'

They commented on the great variety of fish, peering through the steam at the pieces in their bowls.

'She has all scorpion fish,' the brunette announced, indicating the redhead with a wink. 'Now she'll gag.'

'Don't be absurd!' the concierge scolded her. They all laughed and started to eat. She removed the empty tureen, closing the door behind her.

'She is a real treasure,' the first whore declared.

'She understands our difficulties' said the redhead. The first whore glanced at her sharply. 'I meant,' she added, trying to explain, 'at the moment we have a few little financial worries. It is only normal.'

The first whore turned to him with a wide smile: 'We have only been here a week'.

He nodded: 'A whorehouse and *bon ton* don't go together.'

'Bravo!' she said mockingly. 'What do you know about it? And then, even if we haven't lost our good manners that doesn't mean we're not good at our profession.'

He shrugged and said, 'I could be wrong ...' and the subject was dropped. The fish soup took everyone's full attention because of all the bones, but he found it truly delicious. They ate in almost complete silence. Every so often the first whore, speaking as she did, that is with her eyes, offered him inscrutable courtesies between one spoonful and another. It embarrassed him and made him wary. 'What does she want?' he asked himself.

Outside the window the night raged full of lightning and bursts of rain, with thunder booming ever louder. After the soup was finished, a big cake arrived on the table and then coffee.

'Yes, it's true!' said the first whore, offering him a piece of cake. 'I must admit that things are not going quite as one hoped.'

'I see!' he said just to say something as soon as a peal of thunder rumbled off enough to make himself heard.

His conversation with the first whore was becoming so rarefied and fragmented by the roaring storm that it seemed to contain dramatic allusions to matters obscure and solemn such as life and death and suchlike momentous issues which actually made their presence felt from time to time in the room, unspoken but unsettling.

And where do I get the hints from? he pondered irritably. It's time to change key.

But the mood persisted. Almost as a comment on this persistent basso continuo, he saw the brunette extend her arm towards the centre of the table to reach for the coffee-pot; and he found the contrast between her pale bare arm with its supple resolute movement and the still whiteness of the tablecloth extraordinarily seductive. Looking at her closely now, he felt that all her body, even in the smallest movement, was darkly sumptuous, with an insistence on the low notes like a sad refrain, savage and lascivious.

'All right,' he finally said. 'You have some money problems. But isn't that always true at the start of any new business?'

She agreed, but in the conditional mood, expressed with her hands and her eyes more than with her voice; and they continued to converse, sometimes raising their voices above the din of the storm and then lowering them even more than necessary, almost as if sharing secrets.

'You see the two I have,' she said in one of these secret moments. 'One is an innocent, the other is desperate.'

'Why desperate?' he murmured. And between thunderclaps and the downpour he learned that the six-month old baby of the desperate one, presumably the brunette, had been murdered. It seemed they only wanted to kill the husband, but since he was holding the child in his arms both had perished.

'These things happen!' he muttered, consolingly.

But she shook her head: 'They are vicious and craven,' she said. 'Our nation is bizarre: our countrymen combine the bestiality of a savage people with the duplicity and depravity of a civilised one.'

He nodded and suddenly felt that, conjured up in this way during the storm, these traits of his countrymen rose like clouds above the treetops, heading half-way up the mountains and from that height, like destiny, they weighed the country down, which in itself was innocent.

'What about the demon?' he asked to change the subject.

'It's a complicated story!' she said. And she began to tell her tale, in a voice firm and strong against the thundering storm. The demon was a dwarf, fallen or most likely flung out of a train or a circus wagon. Some country people had seen him fly out of the window and roll into a thicket of brambles on the embankment. They had picked him up, brushed him off and gone to call the police. But when the police arrived the dwarf had disappeared. She had come across him two days later in the cellar where he had managed to get through a broken grate over a basement window. This time however he didn't run off, but made signs of wanting to eat. He was not mute, but spoke no language they could understand, except for a very few words they could recognise, picked up from one language or another. She had kept him with her because he was good-natured and cost her little, not needing much food and even less wine. 'He's a balls-grabber!' the redhead had announced several times during the story.

'Well, yes!' the first whore admitted at the end. Sometimes he does grab men by the balls and start to yank on them. In five days I have only seen him do it twice, and only to people who threatened us. One even pulled a knife on me.'

'So then,' the redhead interrupted enthusiastically, 'The demon stuck a hand between his legs and grabbed him from behind and hauled him backwards all the way to the door and threw him into the street.'

'Good,' he commented. 'A chivalrous gesture, I'd say. Why do you call him the demon?'

The first whore laughed: 'In these cases I think he has been an angel, but it seems they called him the demon even when he was working in the circus because of his bad habit of snapping off balls.'

'And then,' the redhead added, 'he only answers to this name. We have tried others like Cheeky Cuntlicker, which would seem more appropriate to this place, but it seemed to offend him.'

'I don't like this story,' the brunette said sulkily. 'Anyhow, I want more coffee.'

'Then you won't sleep!' the first whore warned her.

'She should spend some time in the mountains,' said the redhead, casting a protective eye over the brunette; and she began to discuss the benefits of mountain air. Once, she said, someone had taken her to a hotel by a lake. They had spent three days there and then travelled through the valleys. A week in all. And although no one paid attention to her, she continued to talk almost to herself, but so persuasively that finally all other conversation ceased and even the sounds of the storm seemed to recede. Everyone had another piece of cake and almost without realising it they started listening while she described dawn over the lake, the white water and the shreds of mist, and high on the mountainsides at sunset remote houses perched precariously on the brink between light and night; or late evenings in the valleys when the shadows have arrived almost everywhere, growing denser and darker, while the mountains seem to loom larger with their secret paths, their trees black and thick, their mysterious herbs.

'She speaks well! She doesn't sound the least bit stupid!' he whispered, leaning towards the first whore.

The redhead evidently overheard him and broke into raucous mocking laughter: 'She used the word innocent, not stupid,' she said. 'This is also my speciality as a prostitute.'

'Really!' he stammered. 'So long as we know.'

The first whore laid a hand on his arm, telling him something playful with her eyes, but considerate.

'Now it's your turn to tell us about your big jaw,' the brunette demanded. 'Why is it so white? Couldn't you grow a beard on it?'

'It is white because of vitiligo,' he said, assuming a smugly patient manner, 'and beards can never grow on vitiligo. What's more,' he went on, to forestall other obvious comments, 'it's not easy to chop off a lantern jaw: there is the neck behind, with veins, nerves, muscles, and so forth. Satisfied?'

'Is vitiligo contagious?' the brunette persisted.

'No,' he reassured her. 'It is a skin blemish, congenital like other blemishes: the red ones and the black. This one is white, that's all.'

Suddenly a discontent with everything about himself, in detail and in general, made listening to himself repellent to him. I mustn't speak, I mustn't say another word, he kept mentally repeating, while he went on to relate episodes in connection with his jaw, apparently in excellent humour. 'Once,' he recounted, 'the concierge in a building near our house gave me one of her husband's socks, cut in half and stitched up at the bottom so I could pull it over my chin. "Here you are!" she said to me, "Put it on, but don't let anyone know I gave it to you!".'

'And did you put it on?' all asked in chorus.

'Of course,' he said. 'I was six or seven years old, and I liked the woman: she only really wanted to be kind. She had a daughter a year or two older than myself, who would touch my chin with a finger every once in a while and ask: "Does it hurt?" In other words, they were affectionate people.'

The door opened and a dwarf about three feet tall with a plump face that nevertheless looked extraordinarily stern, approached the table, followed by a little man who was also plump, but smiling, almost scoffing.

'He wanted to announce me!' this little man said, pointing to the dwarf who had taken up a position behind his chair and shifting his face from side to side, gazed up at him with a glum frown.

'What do you want?' he finally asked, with irritation.

On closer examination the dwarf, for all his earnestness or gloom, also looked composed, almost formal and not as ridiculous as one might expect a dwarf to be. He was wearing a dark blue double-breasted coat, a white shirt buttoned up to the neck without a tie, and dark trousers with stripes. His round puffy face looked pinned between the eyes at the root of the nose forming a central point towards which his entire physiognomy contracted or conversely, expanding in folds. Although he had a thick crown of black curls with just a few white hairs, a bald spot showed in the centre, and the bare skin was not white or pink, but grey.

'Damn it, how ugly we are!' he exclaimed, and they all burst out laughing, including the new arrival. Only the dwarf did not laugh, but growled, or rather curled his lips back like a dog, silently showing two rows of yellowish broken teeth.

'Don't fret!,' the new arrival intervened. 'He is growling to make himself handsome'.

'Hmm!' he said, with a shrug. In the meantime the new arrival had drawn up a chair, and seating himself at the table between the first whore and the brunette, almost opposite him, was now regarding him with an alluring smile.

'I know you,' he finally said, 'not personally but by reputation. Hearsay.'

'Really?' he asked. 'And what have you heard them say?'

'Things everyone says,' the other retorted with a wave of his hand. 'Pay no attention! Idle chatter'. He had the hectoring and condescending sneer of one who is too wise to concern himself with the details of existence, but is disposed to tolerate the futility of others.

'And who does he think he is?' he thought, irked by that attitude of philosophic superiority.

'And you,' he asked in the most aloof voice he could muster, 'what do you do?'

The other burst out laughing. But it was a deliberate laugh, a well-rehearsed performance.

'The professor,' the first whore hastily intervened, 'stops by here every so often.'

'This our friend can understand by himself,' the other said, shaking his head. 'As for myself,' he said turning towards him with a politeness that did not seem at all polite, 'I don't do anything in particular, but some people say I have done one thing and others that I have done another and I let them have their say. Take the title of professor, for example. Should I perhaps explain that I never went to school? Not to university, not even elementary school? Too much work. Let them call me what they like. Broadly speaking, I believe that what the living say is always purely momentary, without importance: *flata vocis*, and in this world, in one way or another, everyone breathes his last sooner or later. As for the dead, who can stop them? What the dead say is what they have written and *scripta manent*, as the adage goes. In short, we'll never be free of the dead, believe me.'

'I understand,' he said laughing. 'You favour the classics: Latin? Greek? Is it time to say again: Who will free us from the Greeks and Latins?'

The other used both his head and his hands to refute this: 'No. It is not a classic case: it's a case of lottery numbers: Dead man speaking is ninety; also fear is ninety. People fear wise men because they only speak after death. Your father was a wise man since all can see that you live and prosper.'

'That's true, that's true!' he affirmed.

They both laughed and when their laughter subsided the whispering between the brunette and the redhead could be heard in the silence. The first whore said nothing as if withdrawn into herself. The storm had eased and the night seemed to pass calmly and slowly.

'It feels almost like a family, he thought, except that appearances were concealing something mysterious or, more probably, he thought, something ugly, harrowing or even menacing. He reviewed the figures round the table. The first whore? The ample redhead? Certainly not! Even the beautiful brunette did not seem to wish to hide anything, and the new arrival, although he strove to give himself credit for dark mysterious revelations post mortem, in reality was just a ham actor struggling to play a part too subtle for his coarse nature. The dwarf? He was still perched on his chair at one corner but was no longer gazing at him. In a certain sense he was gazing at everyone and at no one in particular, the way dogs can be at rest without ceasing to be vigilant.

'Hey there, Demon!' he called out, but did not get even a growl in response.

He clapped his hands several times, still with no success while the first whore's eyes went swiftly back and forth between himself and the dwarf, as though following the progress of a game she found only mildly interesting. Of course, he thought, looking at her almost with gratitude, 'the beautiful woman with the eloquent eyes. But suddenly, behind the compliant play of smiles and behind the dreamy clarity of those green glances, he sensed a tenacious silence. It was as if within or alongside the explicit gaze which went around the world lay another gaze directed at the unseen interior of things: a look black with smoky questions, so to speak, in which he recognised at once the mute meditations of his imaginary lover-whore. Nubila et inania, but now seemingly more tender than before.

Bah! he thought, all whores are alike. And since the professor seemed to be looking at him with excessive interest, he called across with a laugh: 'Do you by any chance work at the cemetery? I mean, all this interest of yours in the dead, is it something to do with your profession? In other words, professor, what do you profess? Grave digging?'

Again the professor laughed with evident effort: 'What are you saying? Do I look the funereal type to you?' he asked, thumping his paunch; and after a questioning look around the room received no response he went on with forced merriment: 'Well, why not? Certain funerals are enjoyable if not downright amusing. Just think: the heirs so solemnly festive, the false condolence of friends. No? Certainly there are sad funerals as well: those with white caskets, for example, also because no one inherits from children. But to make up for that, how romantic they are, how moving, how interesting. There is always something entertaining about a good funeral.'

'That's enough!' the brunette shrieked suddenly jumping up, and everyone turned to look at her.

'It's because of what I was saying to her,' the redhead explained hurriedly. 'She's angry at what I said.'

'They are always quarrelling' the first whore commented, shaking her head. She was already on her feet as well, and going over to the brunette she put an arm around her. 'Come!' she said, protectively.

The dwarf rolled off his chair and went to the door to open it, politely standing aside for the two women. Then he followed them out, shutting the door behind him.

'Damn!' he said, banging a hand on the table. 'A fishbone's stuck in my throat. It's been there for an hour and still won't go down.'

'Try swallowing a piece of bread,' the redhead suggested. 'That's what I always do.'

'Of course,' he said. He grabbed a piece of cake and started gulping it down in big mouthfuls. He was not happy about the fishbone invention, the more he thought about it. It was quite obviously a cover-up for some lie. But covering or concealing what? How contaminating! he thought irritably, looking askance at the professor; it seemed to him that the other man's words, under the general heading of 'farce' could pass from the one who had actually uttered them to the one who had simply heard them, or more generally from one author to another. Genres are powerfully confusing, he reflected: as a child he had thought Plautus and Terence was a single name, almost like an impersonal comic authorial brain. Certainly the other man's babble was a series of inanities, fully belonging to the category of human stupidity as a common faculty of thought. But, he asked himself with growing alarm, how many other faculties do we possess in common?

'She's not sick by any chance, is she?' he asked, to break the silence.

'No,' the redhead replied. 'She's only a bit delicate.'

'She wants everybody at her feet,' the professor intervened. 'All beautiful women are like that, even whores.'

'She didn't strike me as particularly beautiful,' he said, 'but I realise that perhaps she is, now you mention it.'

'She's extremely beautiful!' the redhead affirmed heatedly.

He laughed. 'You don't seem envious,' he said.

The redhead shrugged without replying.

Silence returned. 'I'll go and see,' the redhead said at a certain point in a vaguely questioning voice, rising from the table but remaining where she was, looking from one man to the other.

'Well, then go!' he finally said impatiently. She hurried out of the room.

'What a strange place,' he commented, when the door had closed. 'Is it really a brothel?'

The little man made a face: 'Absolutely!' he said. 'A genuine brothel in the old style, although it could also be considered a private club.'

'What do you mean?' he asked.

'The women here,' he explained, 'are given regular medical inspections, which used to be standard procedure. So it wasn't right for you to ask if the brunette was sick.'

'I didn't mean in that sense,' he said. 'I was trying to understand why the others were running after her. Is it pity?'

The other eyed him quizzically: 'Pity?' he asked. 'Here beauty is a virtue and like every virtue it wants to be courted. Of course it is all theatre to a large extent: the "most beautiful" has always played her part in a brothel of quality. And yet there is also a certain spontaneity, sincerity ... Don't you agree?'

'And are you one of the courtiers?' he asked.

The other raised his eyebrows disdainfully: 'I detest virtue,' he declared. 'Ask around.'

'As if I care,' he commented, laughing. 'But tell me,' he went on, 'the truly immense rooms, the medical attention you were talking about and all the rest could be costly and with the pace of business I've seen this evening they can hardly be making much money. In other words, they have good reason to be worried!'

'Don't you fret,' the other laughed, 'more money is coming in than you think. This is a dead time. You can't judge from this. Later the place becomes a gambling den as well ... and then here the whores run no risks because they have no costs: they only pay a percentage of their earnings.'

'Strange,' he said. 'I didn't think prostitution was still good business.'

'It's actually not,' the other agreed. 'But this isn't a money-making concern. It has a more social function, recreational so to speak. In a town like ours, whatever you may think of it, at least the people of quality feel a need for something less materialistic, more disinterested.'

They went on discussing the brothel, the financial arrangements necessary to keep it going, without him having any interest in the conversation whatsoever: it was just talk, he admitted, for appearance's sake. Of course this was one of the most stupid motivations imaginable, but since he could find no other he was compelled to suppose that possibly as an impersonal imperative it was capable of substituting any personal interest of his and even, at least temporarily, his own person, just going on conversing and babbling in his place! Alas, he said to himself, eyeing at his interlocutor almost with repugnance, what will one not do to avoid feeling lonely! But, he reasoned, if at this moment he himself could be said to be absent, replaced by this impersonal imperative interest in keeping up appearances, then it was necessary to think not so much about a self on holiday as about a self deep in its burrow hidden in a solitude more ferociously desperate than that common to all men: they at least have the company of their own words, spoken or thought as the case may be. All of which, he concluded, implied he was so alone he wasn't even with himself.

This final paradox amused him and he began to chuckle, delighted also by the fact that his laughter provoked first astonishment and then apprehension.

'Don't worry, professor,' he exhorted him, looking him straight in the face. But the exhortation did not soothe the professor: it actually seemed to enrage him, although looking livid and clenching his teeth he forced himself to conceal it, chuckling in his turn.

'You have no worries and I quite understand you,' the man finally commented. 'With so many people concerned for your well-being! – Ah,' he said, jerking his head brusquely towards the door, which had silently opened just a crack behind him. 'Here's the vile dwarf back again!' Indeed the dwarf was now trotting towards his corner and his chair, onto which he hopped without losing any of his sullen composure. 'You see how contrite he looks? He's back from the adoration.'

'What adoration?' he asked, laughing in his turn without knowing why.

'Sshh!' the other said putting a finger to his lips mockingly. 'He is in love with the brunette.'

They both went on laughing loudly. 'And yet,' he said after a pause, 'I find the idea of a dwarf as lover grotesque; it shows no respect for the dwarf. Don't you see how solemn he looks?'

'You are quite right,' the professor admitted, 'but I was using lover in the sense of one who loves, not as one who makes love.' He turned in his chair, surveying the dwarf long and hard. 'He is dangerous,' he concluded, resting his elbows on the table again. 'Would you like to know something? Anyone who wants to get to the brunette first has to beat up that shit of a dwarf.'

'*Enfoire*!' the dwarf shouted distinctly, without disturbing a wrinkle on his frowning face. They both laughed.

At this point the first whore entered in a great state of alarm: '*Malin*! ...' she commanded pointing a finger peremptorily towards the door. '*Va-t'en*!'

Without a word the demon rolled off his chair and with the same silence and dignity he'd shown when on entering, he vanished into the darkness beyond the door. The first whore closed it. 'They are staying in the other room,' she said with a sigh. 'They ask to be excused.'

'In that case, we may as well leave too' he said, but without showing any sign of moving.

Instead the professor stood up. 'Well,' he queried, wobbling on his legs, 'are you coming?'

'But why?' the first whore intervened. 'They will be back in a minute, as soon as she has calmed down. You know how she is,' she said turning to the professor. 'She gets her feathers ruffled, but she is a first-class girl.'

'How can you say that!' the man scoffed. 'Big-bum will give her TB with all the effort of continually bedding her.' He brushed aside the hand the first whore stretched out to him and flung the door wide. He vanished without closing it, his footsteps sounding strangely uncertain on the stairs. The first whore closed the door, shaking her head and seemingly upset.

'Everyone is jumpy this evening,' he said, rising in his turn.

'No no,' she said, putting out a hand as if to stop him. 'Now I'll get the brandy. You don't intend to offend me, do you! Would a brandy suit you?'

'The storm has died down,' he objected.

She motioned to him to be silent, took a bottle and two glasses from the sideboard and set them on the table, seating herself opposite him.

'Now let's see,' she said. 'This evening you could devote a bit more of your time to us. We barely know each other.'

He looked at her.

'Devote my time?' he asked. He shook his head. That isn't what one says in a brothel, he thought, disturbed and suspicious.

'All right,' he went on, 'what do you want to know about me? My greatest concern is sleep; and yet I can never manage to, at least not the way I would wish. Do you sleep soundly or do you prefer to stay up late?'

'Who wants to stay up?' she asked. Of course no one can stay awake all night without thinking for instance about all the filth that surrounds us. There is nothing to be done, we're told. We are fucked and our breath is getting shorter, our hearts ache and our stomachs turn.'

'That's how it is, that's exactly how it is!' he approved.

'But in that case,' she continued, laughing, 'we have to recognise that if we despair for the future of this country and therefore want to forget it all by sleeping, what's required is a far deeper sleep: a big sleep in the style of Jacopo Ortis. But speaking for myself ,' she added with a smile, 'I have a tender and trembling heart. Frankly I am afraid, and at this point I prefer insomnia.'

'It's strange,' he said. 'Everything is very strange in this brothel, if you want to know what I think.'

'Perhaps,' she admitted, 'we haven't yet found the right tone.'

'Oh no!' he went on, 'everything is strange, not only the tone. For example, why did that man talk about those two as if they were lovers? Are they?'

She shrugged: 'They love each other,' she said. 'This much is certain. I think they like to take their minds off things by chatting together, that's all. They talk about towns, mountains, lakes. They promise each other great journeys and then feel sad, because these promises are only pretences, and yet they feel some consolation for having made them. What can I say?' she continued after a moment of painful silence. 'I think that the promises, even those that are clearly sentimental nonsense, at least make a story. So after a while they begin to tell each other tales again. They start from what they promised each other as if it were an actual memory of the past, and on they go like that amid continually renewed consolations and equally renewed sorrows.' Her slight laugh was halfway between pity and distress. 'How silly poor miserable people can be!' she concluded almost to herself. 'And then as you know, lesbian acts, faked or real as the case may be, are a traditional speciality for whores, much in demand today.'

They remained in silence for a short time. He finished his brandy, while she had barely tasted hers. He remembered that during the meal she hadn't even tasted the wine and he found such moderation both irritating and poignant.

'Well,' he exclaimed after a moment of silence. 'I have never equated death and sleep. I am not quite so ambitious myself: perhaps I don't even feel the moral repugnance you spoke of, although my stomach turns too. But in my case it might be due to the dreadful wine I sometimes drink in great quantity, while, as I've observed, this isn't the case with you.'

She smiled: 'Wine doesn't mix with our profession,' she excused herself.

'Of course,' he went on, 'I too believe that in the end the death-sleep you spoke of will come for each of us. If I think about it sometimes with some consolation it is because I am not referring to that profound darkness which conceals the things we do not know, but more modestly just the overture: that monotonous preliminary wail which, like a comforting fable, induces us to pretend that all that has already happened and likewise all that is yet to be, is not cause for hate or rage, but nostalgia. For this, as you see, any sort of sleep is enough, even a little nap.'

'You are right,' she said. 'There is no need to dramatise sleep. Basically nothing is more natural or more simple. It is enough, for a start, to close your eyes. Have you tried counting sheep?'

'I certainly have. Sheep, horses. Not cows! They are too smelly,' he said. He thought for a moment. 'I don't always begin with sheep, but with any sort of thing or event. For example: a man of my height, but without a lantern jaw and therefore neither ugly nor handsome, wearing a swimsuit advances along a trampoline which is actually a horizontal bar above a swimming pool. I find this sight desolate. What significance does it have? I ask myself. I can't walk on a horizontal bar, even as a child I instantly fell off every time I tried. So it is not a possibility and if it is not a possibility for me it has no sense for me. But let's go on. Persisting, the man falls into the pool and starts to swim. This is going better! I say to myself with satisfaction – which is reasonable, because this time I could be there in his place, and if so I would swim much better than he seems to be doing.

'There is another way in which what I see when I am verging on sleep seems reasonable: a certain town for example; one never seen before. I love towns, the trees along the pavements, the shrubs in the parks, dogs and cats sniffing around these shrubs, and then the houses, and then the women (the vulva let's say), and also trees in the forests on the slopes of unfamiliar mountains and the clouds in the sky, either tattered by the wind or travelling compact. And since I love these things, it seems to me they make sense. A sort of faraway sense, and with many shades of meaning, as always with melancholy, but it is still sense. But let's go on, I tell myself, let's do our utmost to hunt down this sleep. And then a sort of silence comes over it all: an added tranquillity, I feel. At first they are almost the same things, those I can't help loving a little and others more practical that all the same with a little effort could represent my actual expectations and therefore have a meaning closer to common sense. But the silence extends; now it no longer seems like space, the space of some panorama before my eyes, but like all time: the time of a day, of a year, an entire life. So silence is the locus of everything, the place in which everything is situated and to which everything is reduced, just as now nothing can anymore be reduced to words. Of course I go on seeing, but nothing has a name, nor a voice. Does this make sense? That's what I want to discover.'

She reached out and took hold of his hand, which was resting on the table. 'Poor sleepless friend!' she said, shaking her head.

'Why do you feel sorry for me?' he asked warily. 'Don't you believe that my intention is within the bounds of reason?'

'Undoubtedly!' she assured him hastily. 'But what kind of sense?'

'Well,' he went on, pacified. 'If it is not a verbal sense or one that can be verbalised, it must be a sense attached directly to things: to this glass for example, or your thigh, without transcending either the thigh or the glass. If you knew how many times I have been speechless at the sight of a woman's thigh.'

There was a longish silence. They could hear door hinges squeak, the opening and closing of some drawer in the convolutions of the building.

'As for me,' she finally said, 'I both believe and don't believe in your metaphysics of immanence. If I believed, however, I would be happy and would have no need to sleep for this happiness; or rather I would have no need to stay awake and life would all be a dream. But how can we keep ourselves from asking in the midst of felicity: *Quid tum*? And that's when transcendence arrives, my friend. With banners flying and out for vengeance.'

'Perhaps,' he said, 'this is why I can't manage to sleep.'

She looked at him with a slight smile. 'What can I say?' she eventually said. 'My bed would be pleased to welcome your insomnia.'

He bowed his head gratefully. 'Thank you. Some time or other I will end up accepting your kind invitation. But now it is late, well into the night, and I have to be on my way,' he said, but without moving.

They both laughed. She poured him a second brandy.

'What a dangerous man!' she said.

'Am I?' he asked astounded.

'Certainly not,' she protested. 'I was talking about the professor.'

He shrugged. 'An old man. An old man who doesn't even know who paid him and consequently has nothing to tell. He himself is free game by now.'

'If it is as you say and he knows it,' she said, 'he behaves with courage, and even arrogance. At times he seems to be cheerful, even festive, I'd say.'

'That's right!' he agreed. 'Festive as a pig at the fair. But let's not talk about him any more. Instead I was thinking: If the brunette is truly beautiful, as everyone says and as I myself am now inclined to believe, I have to say that she carries this beauty awkwardly, like a burden. No,' he said, covering the glass with his hand, 'I don't want any more to drink. I have the night ahead of me. And the night is long, as you know.'

'What do you do at night?' she asked, putting the bottle down.

'Friday night!' he said. 'It is the night between Friday and Saturday that is the problem for me. I have established that every week this is my night of freedom. I don't drink every night, believe me. But what else is there to do at night but drink?'

'Don't make me say obscenities,' she said with a forced smile. 'Among other things I think one can also sleep.'

'Of course,' he approved. 'That is the wisest thing.' He opened his wallet and put about half his money on the table.

'What are you doing?' she said, sounding offended. We invited you and now you are paying?'

'What are you saying!' he protested. 'It is for the brunette. Buy her a little dress, a ribbon for her hair, something she might like. Tell her that even Chalky Chin is one of her courtiers.'

'In that case you are very generous,' she said, glancing at the money. 'Do you always go around with so much money on your free night? You seem to be afraid of nothing.'

He smiled patiently. 'With my appearance,' he said, 'others are more likely to be afraid of me. And now,' he concluded, standing up. 'I'll take a walk and get some fresh air. It is good for you after brandy, they say. And now the night seems quiet. It might be possible to see the stars.'

She took his outstretched hand between both of hers. 'In these times,' she said, 'a nasty encounter is always possible, even for people of your build.'

He shook his head.

They had gone out onto the landing at the top of the stairs, and save for the band of light from the open door of the dining room they were in the dark. He could hear the noisy trample of paws coming from somewhere.

'But where do you keep that beast?' he asked.

'I'll go down and turn on the lights,' she said. 'The switch only works from below. Don't move.'

Instead he groped his way down the stairs and on the bottom step the light went on and he found himself face to face with the first whore. He gazed at her for a full minute in silence, trying to imprint her features on his mind. 'I might not manage to remember her!' he thought.

# ACCORDING TO THE RULES THAT GOVERN THE BRINK OF SLEEP

Perhaps all he needed to do was go home and stretch out on his own bed to fall sound asleep. But if he wanted to go back to his apartment he would have to cross the same square again, follow the same streets along the same pavements over the same crossings he had already traversed innumerable times. The topography of this return, clear in its most minute details, to a certain extent formed some part of his sleep. To a certain extent also what was going on around him now as he sat at a table almost in the middle of an immense room, if not actually part of his sleep, seemed to be a prelude to sleep which sometimes insinuated itself into his hypothetical sleep with unpredictable variations, according to the rules that govern the brink of sleep. Certain moments the people there were extraordinary, when he saw them with only one eye and heard them with only one ear, the other being covered by the hand on which his head was resting. For example, sometimes strange groupings occurred: people whose clothes were so brightly coloured they set light circulating between them and other groups with more sombre clothes which gathered shadows. Certainly this cafe bar was full of the sort of people, both men and women, who frequent places that stay open late: cold figures with elusive features but with an appearance that evoked the most bizarre connections. Sometimes just a single figure in front of him in a pose that seemed remarkable in some way, a woman dressed in yellow leaning towards her escort, or a man getting up from a table, was, according to the rules that govern the brink of sleep, enough to cast a different light on some phase of his way home, locating it perhaps through association in a different time of his own past: one summer, for example, close to a tree thick with leaves, the sight of a stretch of pavement caught in the enchantment of the immutability of memory presented itself again in inexhaustible detail. Even with his eyes open to the bustle of the room he could describe the pattern of those slabs of pavement, their shapes, their cracks, where they had sunk under excessive weight so that they collected puddles when it rained. In one of these past seasons, perhaps autumn, the door to his building had been repainted dark green, and now because some voice in his vicinity rose to a harsh pitch he saw this door again shining with fresh paint in the midst of the moonlit night. Certainly there was also a moon tonight; he had seen swollen black clouds swirling around a huge moon, as if taking their leave of her. Now the sky ought to be clear and bright.

'Was it raining when you arrived?' he asked the man who had recently sat down at the table next to his.

The man turned to him with a questioning look, allowing his eyes to settle on him in a long lazy inspection: 'No,' he finally said with a shrug.

The man had a certain solidity about him: thick black hair cropped in military fashion, shabbily shaved, tiny blue eyes under bushy brows and a flat crooked nose. There was also something crooked about his mouth which drooped to the left and indeed the general cast of his features bore with dignity the scars of past battles. He sat bolt upright with his weight firmly planted on his backside.

'Civil questions require civil answers!' he admonished him, and went on to explain that when he asked a question he expected exhaustive replies, ample and detailed responses. How did the sky look? Was the wind blowing? Was the air damp or dry?

The other man looked at him in astonishment: 'Are you trying to start a conversation or are you looking for a fight?' he asked.

He said he didn't mind which: for example he would be perfectly happy to sit and listen if the man wanted to talk about his whore of a wife or he could box his ears if that's what he preferred.

'Just a moment,' the other interrupted him. 'Aren't you the fellow who goes around town hitting waiters?'

'Well,' he admitted modestly, 'on occasion ... only occasionally ...'

The other broke into laughter, complimenting him with nods of approval and finally extended his hand: 'I am a captain,' he said, 'a retired captain.' He added that at the moment he was buying and selling used tractors, and he couldn't talk about his own wife because he was not married; actually he had no family at all so he preferred to go from one hotel to another.

'It's best to be alone,' he agreed; as a matter of fact, he too was alone. He began to cite the advantages of solitude, when an unexpected belch forced him to stop.

The other man looked at him with concern.

'It's nothing,' he reassured him, 'slight inebriation.' He had been drinking all evening, he said, but only intermittently. All in all, perhaps three or four bottles of wine. He didn't like the one on the table now: too much chemical fertilizer. He raised his head abruptly. The other man was listening, nursing his glass without looking at him. He lowered his gaze again to his own glass. The cafe window, he had just noticed, was distant and black as a mirror, blocking out the night. Even if occasional bright flashes scrawled themselves on the sheet of glass there was no way to attribute them to bad weather, but now and again through the constant music from the juke box and over and above the voices he could detect something like the rumble and pounding downpour of a storm which nevertheless could also be the roaring of dishwashers and the rumble of distant flushing. Aside from the sound, though, a whiff of cold air often reached all the way back to his table when the door opened for a moment. At other times a dank smell of mud and damp sawdust pervaded the cafe, lingering in the air and settling on the people: clinging to the skirts of the women he could no longer see now that his head was down but remembered seeing a while before some wandering from table to table, all heavily made-up, and all with bluish circles under their eyes and a darkly ultramarine gaze. A storm, he deduced, was therefore probable.

In any case, the conversation with his neighbour had apparently ended and nothing seemed interesting about the interweaving of murmurings, conversations, and female movements around him, so he returned to his imaginary path home. The door to his building, shining with fresh paint, especially disturbed him because of its resemblance to another door he had seen somewhere earlier, an alien door located in another part of town. He could tell at a glance that in front of that dreadful door, similar in design to his own but located elsewhere, had he felt ill or even dropped dead it would have remained indifferent, obstinately fixed on its hinges without opening even a crack. Of course his own door, although freshly painted, seemed undoubtedly more obliging to him. It retained a certain homeliness acquired in the course of years of use, and despite its new paint continued to open and shut as meekly as before. In his absence, on the other hand, apart from dutifully serving the other inhabitants of the building, it stood there shining, steadfast in its own solitude which, although obviously different from human solitude, was not hostile or aloof like that dreadful alien door with the identical colour and design. In other words, no matter how silly it seemed, he had to admit that his own door by now felt fondly familiar to him.

Looking at things from another angle, or rather thinking about them again let's say six hours later or possibly less, 'familiarity' seemed to depend on shared attributes. For example: melancholy could be attributed as much to himself as to the door, whether closed and shiny, or half-open. In the latter case the desolation within the darkness of the entrance hall could be glimpsed through the crack in the door and a spontaneous question arose: What for? That is: why keep going in and out, why keep on opening and closing; why these frequentatives in which duration was chopped up, as much for the door as for him?

In principle, he didn't mind this adjectival partnership between himself and things because these things seemed to have acquired, through the shared adjectives, the power of living in his stead, thus sparing him the efforts and risks of existence, so he could simply marvel. In addition, he could say that the more the subject migrated from himself towards things, so much more restful or slow his own thinking became. The gratitude or the affection that he felt for certain objects was simply a reflection of the extent of this lazy mental tranquillity.

Only in principle, he added, only in a most general way. In reality, on the contrary, day by day and hour by hour, this condition of partial and provisional release from himself was merely a confused and exasperating yearning: he slept so rarely and for such brief periods of time that although his mind sometimes approached the serenity of aimless thinking he never attained that serenity but only moved in a direction he hoped might end in sleep. When fully awake, on the other hand, this fabled tranquillity was merely a nebulous hypothesis midway between desire and memory, barely distinguishable from other half-memories or inconclusive daydreams. The past, or rather what might have already happened (perhaps without having actually happened) was the favourite setting for his possessives: 'his' doorway, 'his' slipper, 'his' tree, 'his' crow ...

Fancy that! he thought, struck by the last example. How does a crow come into it?

Rummaging through his baggage of memories, discouraged and weary even before the search began, at a certain point nevertheless with a sigh of relief he retrieved the crow. Actually he had seen not just one but a number of crows somewhere perched in a bare tree, all but forgotten now save for the way they continued to gleam even with the wind blowing in violent gusts and sudden squalls of rain, defiantly contemplating the turbulent horizon. One could say, from the example of the crows, that he loved tremulous memories, memories that lacked stability and yet persevered. Having reached this conclusion and being about to close this train of thought, at least for the time being, a doubt arose about another feature of the possessive: fastened to his face or rather to his lantern jaw. Could it be called his, this jaw, or rather did it not stand in for him as an emblem or symbol of his presence, so that whenever people in town saw this lantern jaw they expected to find him there too, even if he himself was momentarily distracted or at least mentally far away?

'How about little old men?' the man at the table on his right, who had introduced himself as a retired captain, interrupted him.

He looked at him with surprise: 'What do you mean, captain?'

The other explained that he wanted to know if he also hit old men. According to him, this was an interesting question because he had known some old men who seemed to have great trouble staying upright, and as a result their balance seemed more a result of meditation than posture. In other words, they had seen what they had seen and now despite the spectre of these past visions, they went around holding themselves upright with precarious dignity. If one were to ask: 'How did life treat you, old-timer?' they would reply, carefully positioning their feet but with no other hesitation: 'Not so bad, not so bad!' Yet surely at this point giving a mendacious old man a clout over the ear would have been just and edifying.

He approved but said he always chose people who were solid and steady on their feet so as to avoid paying damages and not risk having even more serious problems with the law. From this point of view, waiters were convenient, also because they didn't count. *De minimis non curat praetor.*

The captain praised him for his prudence and so he went on to explain that his choice was not limited to waiters but also included colleagues or rather subordinates in the office, cleaners, or tram drivers, a postman or two, if he remembered correctly. Thinking it over, it seemed to him that his choices were essentially opportunistic, prompted by the position of an individual head or the shape of a neck, wherever he chanced to find them. In fact he had even whacked some people who frequented bars although at the moment he wasn't able to say exactly who, because he usually paid more attention to necks and the backs of heads than to faces. 'You see,' he said, 'a good whack is delivered with the open hand between the head and the neck usually from right to left and slightly from below, but always from behind, so as not to spoil the element of surprise.'

'That's true,' the captain nodded. 'I actually saw you at work two or three nights ago when you started to hit the bald waiter at the Cafe della Posta. Two strikes in a row, one from the right and the other from the left in that case. Isn't that how it was?'

They both laughed, although he didn't recall that hitting the bald waiter had been particularly amusing. What this episode did call to mind however was the white napkin the waiter carried on his arm which had remained almost immobile on the sleeve of his black jacket throughout the jolts following each blow. Even afterwards in the torrent of shouts and abuse he could again see the cursing waiter's face blaze red right up to the top of his bald head while he kept jumping up and down at a prudent distance, occasionally pretending to want to launch himself at him. And the white napkin remained limp and calm, symbol of indolence and peace in the late November afternoon, pervaded by the light of a serene sunset.

'Where do you usually eat?' the captain asked him.

He replied that when he was out and about he ate wherever he happened to be, not really caring. Besides, when he was roaming around he didn't eat much because wine, especially bad wine, took away his appetite. He usually stayed at home, trying to sleep, and in that case he ate tinned beans and chickpeas, sardines packed in oil too, and also biscuits, oranges, and bananas by the dozen. Since he could never get to sleep he sometimes managed to devour up to six pounds of fruit a night. He described his apartment, or rather the part in which he was living at the moment. There was a kitchen, he said, but he never used it. He ate without plates, directly from the tin, using only a fork and a newspaper for a tablecloth. He had so many useless things: books, hair driers, a typewriter, slippers.

And speaking of slippers, it suddenly occurred to him that they, as much or perhaps more than his front door, were sentimental ingredients of his life, things to love with a love that might admittedly be feeble and intermittent, not least because they had not been used as slippers but kicked around the room until they ended up taking refuge, one under one piece of furniture, the other under another. These days of kicking slippers around were empty days and slow to pass, endless summer evenings burdened with a slovenly and almost shrewish solitude which was utterly familiar. Where did this solitude come from? Roughly speaking so long as solitude simply coincided with his happening to be alone, that is something as spontaneously natural as sleeping alone, then it could be said that things tended to go fairly smoothly. Perhaps in the summer if it was very hot he and solitude slept an exhausted sleep together, weary and so oblivious that they were almost a single thing. But suddenly the awakening would come, or rather, because he had not actually been asleep but had merely allowed himself to start thinking in an irresponsible way, as one lonely person to another, he'd leap out of bed saying: 'But what is this?' That is, in the white light of reason his relationship with himself appeared like a text rehearsed to death, and now one could see with pitiless clarity its sloppiness and heartbreaking mediocrity. 'Ah, it's made of brass,' he said to distract himself, looking at the antiquated chandelier overhead with increasing pity.

'In other words, things are as they are,' he said to conclude his description of his quarters, 'I also have a mirror in the bathroom that is useful when I shave.'

The captain complimented him vaguely and immediately went on to discuss the wine with an almost bookish competence.

'You know,' he said after a while, interrupting him. 'My building has a front door. And now they have painted it green.'

'Really?' the other replied. They looked at each other questioningly for some time, without finding anything more to say. Then he lowered his eyes to his glass, feeling uncomfortable that he had started to divulge something without knowing how to go on, when suddenly he seemed to comprehend that these doors and slippers were all variations on an image that was broader and incomplete, but which he had actually already seen and which he therefore believed he could begin to describe. So, leaving aside the chandelier and other everyday objects or incidents, one evening when he happened to be looking through the kitchen window he noticed a large block of flats about thiry metres away, simpler than the one in which he lived, and higher up, built on the hillside. Anyhow, between the two buildings, (or rather between the back of his own and the front of the other), was a derelict steep terrain with tufts of weeds and brambles crossed by dirt paths, and without being filthy it looked distinctly pitiful. The building itself shared that same open sloppiness. Its facade was defaced by countless medium-sized windows: forty-eight or possibly more, almost all of them open, with yellow or green curtains dangling askew. There were white cardboard boxes on some of the windowsills, twig brooms were jutting out of others, and everything faced flatly west, straight into the blazing sunset. So there was all that white with windows and in that white the immense shining evening heading inevitably towards the night which would conceal it, obliterating its reality; but for the moment the squalor of that ugly building shouted out defiantly that it was still as it was. What for, my God? he asked himself. And the word 'God' in his question filled him with sorrow, associated as it was with the misery of subsidized housing, and the sour smell of brooms and mops set up to dry for hours at the window in the afternoon sun. It must be this, he said to himself. Solitude lines up too many things without true consequentiality, blurring the logical links like a dream. Images that are parenthetical or marginal in vigilant thought become an integral part of the sequence of a dream the way a dreamer can go down into the cellar and as he goes down the stairs see the foundations of the building and the way they were assembled stone by stone: the dreamer sees the workers laying the stones even if they died two hundred years before, and watching these earnest workers, busy despite their death, the dreamer understands with a tug at his heart what it is that gives rise to that gratitude and affection that sometimes is felt for the unknown and for the silence of the things that surround us: for front doors or in his case for slippers, or even for the furniture which remained cloaked in dust-sheets in that part of the flat he had not entered for three years. Why such abandon? one wonders. And extending one's gaze to all the things one has seen, all the moments which will never be repeated when one actually looked at the world, at the sunsets, at the dawns of the most distant past now half-submerged in forgetfulness, one feels how fragile even the glory of the sun may be. The entire world passes from one hour to another without return. And this, he concluded, is such a widespread commonplace that the tenor even sings: *'L'ora è fuggita, io muoio disperato!'* with all that follows.

So let's think about something else, he told himself. Something else, something else! he repeated, letting his head droop over the table under the weight of an increasing distress. He felt, though, that with who knows what cunning he might still be able to get an idea going, a train of ideas, a sequence of thoughts proceeding in the general direction of health: that of the body at least, if not of the soul. A whore, for example. If he could only manage to think back to his first whore, then through a miracle of whorish protection he would at once feel he was elsewhere, far from the dismal smell of the greasy table. Perhaps even a momentary promise of protection would be enough, as if she happened to pass close by, circling and gliding away as swans inexorably glide away on the slimy waters of a lake. And now the water was already visible and soberly at the break of day the whore seemed to move as mysteriously and calmly as a great ship, her poop lit by the dawn, slightly swaying at the hips, breasting the waves that were still black and deserted.

Under his forehead damp with sleep, the table shook from a great thump. Looking up he saw a face blackened up to the eyes by a beard, glaring at him with no sympathy.

'No sleeping here!' the face said, banging down the bottle which he had picked up to wipe the table with a soft threadbare rag.

'Oh, you son of a whore!' he shouted. 'What is this? I was dreaming about your mother and you wake me up. There is no filial piety any more, none at all!'

'No sleeping here!' the man repeated, passing the rag over the table again. He had a bony face and a stern appearance, although huge donkey teeth bulged from his lips in a continuous yellowish sneer.

'Why not beat him up?' the captain at the table on his right suggested confidingly.

'Not now,' he said, hesitantly, 'maybe later'.

And because in the meantime the waiter had moved away towards the middle of the room: 'I don't feel like running after him,' he explained. 'Perhaps if he comes back'.

'Hey, you!' he shouted after him. And when the man already halfway across the room paid no attention, neither turning nor stopping, he flung his empty glass at him striking him hard in the back, but without breaking the glass, which bounced several times on the floor at people's feet.

This time the waiter did turn, almost hopping back, his eyes red and baring his teeth like a donkey about to bite.

'So you can't hear?' he asked, as soon as the man had stopped in front of him.

'I'll call the police!' the waiter stammered.

'Good for you!' the captain approved, 'so the police can shut down this whorehouse for a month.'

The waiter leaned right over him: 'I can always fix your jaw for you. What do you say?' he whispered confidentially.

He straightened himself against the back of his chair, inspecting the waiter from head to foot with approval: 'Would you really fix it?' he asked. 'How much do you want?'

'Jaws?' the captain interrupted. 'Did I hear mention of jaws?'

'Oh, yes!' the waiter said boldly, but already a bit confused. 'I could reduce it by half and there would still be too much of it.'

'Go ahead!' he accepted, closing his eyes.

The waiter swallowed several times. 'But not here!' he said finally, excusing himself with evident embarrassment.

He opened his eyes abruptly. 'You see,' he said gently, 'what a swaggering bastard you are?'

Under the pressure of his shoulders the back of his chair began to creak and split apart. He got up to examine the damage. 'Bring me a stronger chair,' he said. Then he ordered a bottle better than the first, and changing his mind, asked for a brandy: then no brandy, just a simple black coffee, always calling the waiter bastard.

'He is a mule, I'd say,' the captain interrupted sternly. 'You, mule,' he shouted, turning to the waiter. 'If you make me stand up too, I'll ram this bottle up your nostrils!'

This time the waiter took a step backwards, then slowly, almost reluctantly, he turned to leave.

'Poor bastard!' He felt sorry for the man as he walked away limping perceptibly. He was seized by a sense of unease that was all the more intense for being inexplicable. He certainly didn't like someone saying he was going to fix his jaw and then not doing it. But it was normal for things of this sort to happen to him in bars at that time of night. He could have even hit the waiter, calling his wife his daughter his mother and his grandmother all whores, but this had also happened to him at other times in the past and now all these 'other times' made him feel uncomfortable. That was a mistake, he said to himself. A mistake. But was there another way to act? Of course there was, but even this other way, whatever it might be, seemed mistaken. Everything was a mistake, to a greater or lesser extent, and yet certain actions at first appeared to be less mistaken than others, but he had never understood why; and then the minor mistake, the almost right thing, seemed more painful than the completely wrong, because to the uncomfortable feeling was added a sense of remorse and of grief for the missed opportunity. What a muddle! he said to himself. The bar, the waiter, the country, the entire world. We are in the midst of it and don't understand a thing. He shook his head, bored. And yet, he added, perhaps the truth really does exist. Explicit, simple ... Five or six words in all, no more.

'What about you,' he said, turning to the captain, 'do you think about truth?'

'Me?' he said. 'Well, sometimes I do.'

For some while they were both silent, each frowning, in evident mental effort.

'I was thinking,' the captain eventually said, 'that perhaps it might have been better to hit him.'

'Perhaps!' he admitted.

'Another time' they both concluded, almost as one. They glanced at each other, shaking their heads with philosophical forbearance.

All of a sudden the hope came to him that the music, the waiter, this moderately noisy and muddling night were merely distracting interludes recurring according to a fixed timetable between segments of sleep or at least of drowsiness aggravated by fatigue. As in a deserted station after the ticket office closes, when the long drawn-out clatter of entire trains passes through it every quarter of an hour, wagon after wagon (long convoys of night freight whose nature and destination it would be idle to conjecture), the regularity of the intervals between sound and silence, or perhaps the clarity of the contrast between these two events, made both enter into a single logic, as two different words enter into a single idea. Silence and clatter in this case formed one single proposition, but complete and with a restful simplicity that one could enjoy in the middle of the night. 'We travel!' one could say. 'That's all!', thinking with gratitude not only of the station but the town that offered a refuge for this very simple phrase. Perhaps truth, rather than a thing in itself, was a place or situation of fulfillment in which, on arrival, even the most uncertain ideas, the most tangled propositions, sort themselves out with an obviousness it was impossible to doubt. Outside the station therefore, or outside the bar in this case, between intervals of rain or moonlight, churches and monuments were awaiting any idea with marmoreal tranquillity, rendered aloof by their solitude. A solemn expectation no doubt, and an imposing scene, but so persistent that the grandeur and pomp looked more and more like funereal decor or, even worse, evil omens.

'What nonsense!' he said, this time with his voice strong and steady.

'Quite right' the captain commented encouragingly.

He shook his head.

A man and a woman (she was middle-aged, dry and mannish in her haircut and face, he was grey, quiet and stooped) approached the next table and took off their drenched raincoats, placing them on the back of a nearby chair. As she did this, the woman peered straight into the distance in every direction, deliberately ignoring her fellow-man.

'You can talk all you like, but it is just as I say!' she said, sitting down. The man too sat down without a word and an aura of damp and rubber and wet sawdust spread around them. The jukebox music grew louder and louder as the night went on, and the customers too, although their numbers were down, adopted postures that were more nocturnal and almost declamatory. There were enough indications to deduce that it was raining heavily outside and these last hours were hours subtracted from sleep.

'Some of them are even attractive!' the captain said as if talking to himself , 'but they all have short legs.'

They continued for some time to exchange opinions about the women in the place and more generally about those available in town. All had legs that were shorter than average, while the ones who were not paid had normal legs, according to the captain. He, the captain, had once upon a time had a lover with normal legs, but over their ten or eleven years together, that is when he lived in the room that she rented to him, her breasts had become pale and long. He had come to see these breasts steadily growing paler and longer as a bad omen. In the morning, especially in the winter, her breasts forecast cold and rainy days in which he knew he would not manage to do anything but leap from one cafe to another, between the showers and the puddles. In the end he had gone away, leaving that town, leaving the north, but he knew that she was still there, in the fog, with her long breasts laden with portents and omens.

He laughed discreetly and to return this confidence in some fashion he began to tell a foggy story about the first whore he could remember: the first of his life, not very beautiful, rather small and round without being fat. He was always searching for her without ever finding her.

'Who knows what happened!' he concluded.

'Perhaps she moved to another town!' suggested the captain.

'It's possible' he said, but added that perhaps his memory was poor and therefore he could not have recognized her even if he had encountered her.

'But there are whores like that,' the captain encouraged him. 'They're not hard to find. Look at that one, for example.'

He shook his head.

'Did she have brown hair?' the captain began to question. 'Blonde? Her eyes? Her arse? What about her arse? Sometimes it's easier to recognize a whore by her arse than any other feature.'

'This woman has eloquent eyes,' he said. 'That is, no,' he corrected himself. 'That was another one: one I just met this evening.' For a moment he was lost in thought. 'But tell me what does one do with all these characters?'

'Which characters?' the captain asked in return.

'The whores,' he explained, 'and other women: other men, too. In other words the characters in life who appear and then vanish without trace. One would want to know something more about them, but I never manage even to remember their faces.'

The captain nodded: 'I understand,' he said, 'it's like that famous story of the man who reads the telephone book from end to end, thinking it's a novel. "The story of my life", he says to himself.'

They both laughed.

In the meantime nothing happened. Looking around the room, he noticed that the know-all woman and the weary man had vanished from the table on his left. A bedraggled old man approached the empty table, but then seemed to change his mind and wobbled off, trying to get his balance on legs that looked stiff. The waiters evidently had stiff legs too, but for them balance and a certain agility were professional attributes, independent of the state of their legs. Despite so many tiny scattered events, nothing had happened. The facts, if what happened could even be called by that name, happened more because time went by than due to any factual logic: time went by, another hour followed, more nocturnal, more rainy than the previous ones, a chair was moved or a new customer silently crossed the sawdust to the bar. On the other hand, these facts or other similar ones brought to mind the weather, almost as if they belonged to it.

For example, was it raining now? How much rain had he seen

or heard pouring down in his time, year after year, years ago? It could be the same rain, save that this in comparison seemed to him at times less rainy, more like the ghost of some past primal reality, which in any case it would be useless to attempt to recall since the memory of it was by now too confused.

'The truth is,' the captain said incongruously, 'that there are now more whores than church bells.'

'True!' he agreed.

A short time passed. Perhaps it was raining, perhaps not. The window was far away and in any case the shadow of the portico blotted out the night; the bottle was almost completely empty and the glass as well. Yet there was, he admitted, a certain thematic coherence between all these things and the people he saw wandering around the bar in the thrall of a feeling of being incomprehensibly lost. The captain next to him was talking to a small pale-looking young woman and this too was part of the theme, whatever the title of this cursed theme might be.

Maybe it's not a bad idea to talk of a theme, he said to himself. Perhaps it is in the theme that fulfilment should be sought, or the logic of what one sees happening. He looked around and finally, lowering his gaze, he noticed a big button on the floor amid the sawdust and scraps of paper. Stretching out a leg he gave it a little shove with his toe. It was an ordinary mass-produced metal button, probably from a female garment.

His first impulse was to wonder who might have lost it, but on starting this train of thought he quickly discovered it would require effort and lead nowhere. So what? he asked himself. For its part the button lost amidst the trash made its own quiet sense; it was in a theme. The immediate benefit of this belonging to the theme was inertia and with it a certain peace. And yet the same thing could be said not only about the button but about an empty twisted cigarette pack a bit further away, a rolled up newspaper, and leaving the floor and the trash, about glasses and bottles on the tables themselves, and the chairs ... Brought into the theme, all these scattered things could be read in single way which while respecting the distinctions resulted only in a feeling of inertia, ubiquitous like a universal passe-partout.

But the men? The whores? he objected. And yet, he responded with a lump in his throat for the distress, the Messiah has already come! What else can we hope? So this is all and there is no point in complaining! As if cradled between the words 'Messiah' and 'All', almost on the brink of sleep, he looked at the proposition or theme of the already accomplished coming of the Messiah: Peace and profundity! But he was afraid to look too long.

He shook his head in dismay.

'How is it going with the whores?' he asked the captain, who also seemed to be meditating now, with his head bowed over the table.

'Badly, badly,' the captain answered moodily; and without looking at him, went on to mutter curses to himself. 'Do you realize,' he asked suddenly, raising his voice, 'that these damned women get more grasping every day?' He shot him an inquiring look. 'You don't have these worries,' he resumed bitterly. 'Believe me, it is sad to be made to feel poor, as well as old, in the eyes of a whore.'

'Everything costs more nowadays,' he observed, evasively.

The captain nodded grimly. 'Never mind,' he said, suddenly breaking into a laugh. 'It's fun while it lasts.'

The pale-faced woman returned and leaning over him placed both hands confidentially on his shoulders and whispered something in his ear. His face seemed to darken, but he made no reply, and she sat down next to him.

They talked softly for a few minutes. They seemed to get on so well together that for a moment he imagined that they were long-term lovers, a trifle sad, bickering a bit, each accusing the other of the burden of life. Finally the woman stood up, and the captain dismissed her with a pat on the bottom, which struck him as a strangely kind gesture.

'That's how it is,' the captain said, talking to himself. 'That's how it is!' he continued to repeat. He himself wasn't looking at him. He wasn't really looking at anything but the general confusion in the room. Suddenly the doubt crossed his mind that perhaps he only thought he was looking or else that even while looking the interpretive component of his seeing (logic and rules of interpretation, rather than specific interpretations) was gaining ground over the things seen. Now these rules all together showed a marked tendency to the right; that is everything gravitated towards a mental right that had nothing to do with his field of vision but which instead designated a place of growing oppression. He tried to counteract this pull, to combat this tendency by reasoning in ways that in any case he realized were as insidious as they were useless. On the other hand, if this is the result, this is the end, why go on trying to resist? he pondered.

The captain seemed to share none of these preoccupations: he was busy with the women, each looking more pitiful and forlorn than the next. One in particular he felt was a striking image of affliction and distress. Now it was no longer next to the captain he saw her, he remembered that perhaps he had seen her before in a bus station, sitting on a bench in the waiting room. At every announcement from the loud speaker she gathered up her belongings and rearranged them around her on the bench and on the ground: a basket, a bag, a large suitcase. The place was entirely of glass, and drenched with light. The sun, now low behind the trees, poured so much light into the room that there was no appreciable difference between inside and outside the waiting room. The light was exactly the same as the light on the square outside, with the same blue shadows from the trees advancing inch by inch from the exterior towards the interior.

In this certainly exceptional if not strange light the girl unexpectedly looked up at him and then with canine cunning, not moving her head, shifted her gaze to the side, pretending not to have been looking. Those eyes, turned aside to hide the pupils, showed all the white of the eyeballs: a whiteness gleaming like porcelain which presented a false splendour in the sadness of the setting sun, and appeared to be an omen of insanity.

'Dreadful!' he exclaimed. And such was the distress of this memory of his, so unusual and so menacing, that he could no longer continue along the same vein, his thought felt forced to search for another direction. But this is the point: What direction? Towards what thought? Towards the right, towards the left, or perhaps more sagely towards the centre? And even as he pondered these things he realised that he was dangling off his chair towards the right and was just about to fall. With a jolt he regained his balance, or rather stood up as the chair fell to the ground.

Meantime the woman had returned to the captain's table. She sat peacefully next to him, but it was at himself that she was staring.

The woman chortled to herself for a few seconds and then started to laugh openly in a way he didn't find offensive, but friendly and benevolent.

He also broke into laughter: 'It happens to me,' he explained. 'I drop off, without truly sleeping ...'

'Naturally,' she said, 'but if you had a bed ...'

He drew his chair up to their table. 'In bed,' he said, 'I jump almost two feet in the air and land on the floor, sheets, blankets and all.'

The three of them laughed heartily.

'You know what we should do?' the captain suggested. 'Let's get a couple of bottles and all go to her place.'

The woman shook her head: 'I can't,' she said with regret, 'I truly can't.' He too apologized that he couldn't accept, but to rouse the company again he returned to the topic of the quasi-sleep that they had seemed to enjoy. 'You see,' he explained, 'it seems to be sleep: from many signs I can deduce with near certainty that I am sleeping, but the moment I am convinced and start to examine the subject of my supposed dream, the subject explodes into a thousand pieces. My thought comes to a sudden stop like a train crashing into a wall. Boom! And I land on my stomach on the floor. All of this, from closing my eyes to the final thud takes exactly seven minutes on my alarm clock: once it took eight, but that happened only once.'

'Boom!' the woman repeated laughing. 'And do you always land on your stomach?'

'Stop it!' the captain scolded her.

'Yes' he replied in turn. 'Stomach, arse, what difference does it make?'

'Never on your jaw?' she asked.

'What an idiot!' the captain sneered.

'Naughty, naughty!' he admonished her with his finger. All three started to laugh again together.

'Don't be upset,' the woman finally said. 'I didn't say that to hurt you; actually I think that you are an ugly handsome man like a bad actor.'

'All right,' he agreed, 'I'm a bad actor.' After this admission, the conversation languished; the captain actually succumbed to several half-yawns.

'Why don't we order some champagne?' the woman asked several times. And when the captain pretended not to hear, he finally conceded, 'Let's move on to the champagne! Be my guests.'

A waiter different from the one who offered to fix his jaw brought the bottle with great ceremony and demanded immediate payment, claiming he was going off duty, and after some tergiversation while the captain groped in all his pockets without success, he ended up paying for everything: both the champagne and all the wine they had drunk before. He added a good tip and was heartily thanked by all concerned, including the woman and the waiter.

'You are munificent!' the captain said, and then solemnly explained to the woman that munificent was a 'synonym for generous'.

At this point the woman started talking about a dear friend of hers, and since the friend just happened to be passing their table the captain made an athletic leap, grabbed her by the wrist and drew her to the table.

The new arrival was extremely pale, wearing a great deal of make-up and long false eyelashes, one of which dangled over her right eye.

'Why don't you take them off,' he suggested, feeling sorry for her, 'before it falls off.'

As soon as she was seated, the new arrival followed his advice, stowing the eyelashes carefully in a little box and putting it in her handbag. When these operations were accomplished, she looked up at the company. Without the burden of the heavy black lashes her gaze brightened and her face softened.

By this time the bottle of champagne was finished, and another was brought, which also lasted just a short time, and a third followed to encourage the new arrival to talk. But when she finally conquered her innate shyness and spoke no one felt any desire to listen to her apart perhaps from himself who, although stretching and yawning like the others, still could not help listening to her, so resigned and sweet was her voice.

The narrator began by talking about an apartment that she shared with someone who took a certain amount from her for every man she entertained, threatening her with a knife if any payments were not forthcoming. From this story she went on to others, all very confused, about colds, influenza and other illnesses, some of which however she had suffered as a child, before her father died. She was visibly drunk and spoke in a meandering, incoherent way, often contradicting herself and laughing at unsuitable times. Nevertheless, despite the contradictions, as her tale gradually unfolded special days seemed to emerge from the general fogginess of the story. Days in the country, rainy and mild, other strange days full of drunken recklessness, slow days with interludes lived at the brink of unconsciousness, and long wearisome days full of effort searching for a meal, a room, some work. Today she was still looking for work, she said.

'Why work?' he asked. 'Why not just go back to your village?'

Before he had even finished the sentence, the music suddenly stopped and his last words seemed to roll around the near-empty room. The bedraggled old man with the stiff legs was still wandering among the tables, undecided, close to the window which now mirrored his blurred and distorted wandering shadow and looked blacker than ever. The tables were deserted by this time, but two last customers were lingering at the bar to his right. The waiters had vanished and a cleaner had begun to sweep up at the back of the room to his left.

'Fine!' said the captain. The woman laughed. Someone coughed and then it was silent again, with only the rustling sound of the broom against the damp sawdust. Thus an entire minute passed, then another. And as the second minute was about to end, with vague remorse he began to try to recall the events of the evening, from the girl's last words proceeding backwards, without forgetting the part, albeit minimal, that the bottles of champagne had played.

# A REVERSE SUN

One summer in the country an unknown aunt had arrived at the house one afternoon around five. 'You should call her "countess",' they had forewarned him. 'Only "countess", remember, although she will call herself your aunt.' He had subsequently learned she had been married to his mother's brother and after his death had married again, and after this second husband's death she married a draper, no less, who was also dead now.

'What a paradise you have here!' the aunt had said, vaguely gesturing at her surroundings, perhaps the trees in the woods, perhaps the mountains. And they had all smiled, without giving too much importance to her. No one had given her much importance, not even the servants; at supper she had been relegated to a corner of the table and everyone had gone on chatting as usual, almost as if she did not exist. So after supper, standing up and looking about her, she could think of nothing better to do than slip her arm through his, urging him: 'Show me the garden.'

At this range, his aunt's face looked white and slightly shiny, almost like candle wax. Her brown hair, fastened in two tight bands covering her ears, was also shiny but unlike her face the texture was dry and flaky.

'How old are you?' she had asked, turning her face to him.

'Eleven' he had replied.

*'Tiens,'* she said. 'I would have guessed fifteen. You are very tall for your age.'

As they were speaking, they went out onto the portico and stood there while she went on exclaiming, 'What a paradise you have', gazing upon the dark of the night as if it were a sunny panorama. In fact the sky was covered by clouds that blocked out the stars and nothing could be seen around them except for fringes of light on the tops of the trees from distant lightning.

'I must say something to her,' he was thinking, 'but what can I say?' Finally after some doubt and hesitation he had begun: 'Countess ...' But not knowing how to go on, after almost a minute's silence he had blurted: 'Countess, what is life all about?'

She sighed. 'Trouble! Nothing but trouble, my child, especially for someone landed with a lantern jaw like yours'.

And turning her back on him, she returned to the house.

He had stayed alone in the dark, thinking that the incident was neither pleasant nor unpleasant, but that altogether there was something utterly unreasonable about it. From that moment on he had imagined that all unreasonableness or rather anything that resembled nothing else, the utterly strange, just for this radical dissimilarity with any other thing, belonged to a separate genre, not only literary, but as physical as a compartment of space: the same space for clouds and wind; nocturnal space, but crossed by streams of light. In memory, this was the place for his unknown aunt, but also for other memories with no territorial claims. And now, while in the storm the rumbles of thunder grew ever longer, stronger and more frequent, he felt he was in this place of strangeness yet again. He peered at his companions in this windowless room dominated by a skylight pelted with rain with the stunned curiosity with which one regards the miserable marvels of distant lands: two wan unimportant faces sitting in silence, occasionally sipping from their glasses.

I ought to say something to them, he thought. But finding nothing appropriate he merely threatened them once again with his hand.

'It's the worm,' the fatter one burst out, pointing at the figure next to him. 'He keeps farting, saying that with all this thunder no one can hear.'

'I will give you both a good whack if you continue' he said wearily.

The clamour of the storm suddenly struck him as all the louder for its unimportance. 'Let nature take its course,' he said to himself. And since nature found nothing better to do than roll clouds and spill buckets of water all over town, he had no choice but to wait. In the meantime one could do whatever one wanted, provided it was futile or inconsequential, like yawn or sleep; nature in men and nature in the world coincided in the futility of expectation, that is in being other than any reasonable thing. But that was the point: while other men adapted to this gratuitous otherness, sleeping or farting like the worm or turning over in their beds at an especially loud clap of thunder, he alone considered this 'being other' as a real alternative, which as it loomed above the horizon with startling and almost ridiculous sublimity acquired a sort of imminence, and in the meantime not the least intimidated he kept on waiting, unflinching as it were, to see what would happen next.

'What will happen next?' he asked himself. It was actually absurd to think that anything could happen through merely finding himself in the company of who knows what whore-mongers. It was an episode of no consequence, such as could only happen in a place as strange and isolated as this. After all, what consequence could the night-time questioning of an unknown aunt about life, the universe and everything ever have?

'Ah well, he said, 'everyone is asleep at this hour, except for drunks like you.'

'What about you?' the so-called worm interrupted him aggressively. 'If I am still up, it is to offer you hospitality as the proprietor of this establishment.'

'Your profession of pimp is what makes you do it,' the more corpulent one observed punctiliously.

'Shut up, foul toad,' said the worm. 'So what is your profession?'

They continued to argue for some time until they noticed he was watching them without saying a word. Then, by mutual consent, they switched to a more neutral tone and remarked upon the strangeness of the season in general and especially this storm, which, according to the toad, was so violent that it would undoubtedly result in death and injury.

'That's a fact,' agreed the worm. 'If I hadn't been here to give you shelter, who knows what would have become of you two with all this wind.'

'With all the money you've taken, you mean!' the toad cried angrily. 'And where is the whore for example? Tell me, where's the whore? Sleeping! That's handy, isn't it?'

The worm protested that it was not his fault, that she had been fine at the beginning, but then she had got that stomach ache, which might be the result of something she had eaten at the restaurant, or else the moon.

'The moon?' he asked.

The toad started to laugh so hard he even slapped the table twice.

'He's happy!' he commented, turning to the worm with a wink.

'Anyhow,' said the worm, 'why is this vile toad talking this way? "The whore is not here! The whore is sleeping!" It's not nice to say such things. If she had stayed, I was thinking we could have played a bit of poker to pass the time, but since the gentleman doesn't want to play poker it makes no difference whether she is asleep or awake.'

'Quite right,' he agreed. 'No difference.'

'He cadges drinks and then he claims …' continued the worm. 'If this ugly toad is safe under my roof, it is all due to you wanting to pay for his bottle as well.'

'And what a good bottle!' sneered the toad.

He observed him more closely; in fact at a certain point, to get a better look at him, with his foot he shoved the man's chair away from the table, closer to the light, which came from a bare bulb dangling on a wire against the wall on his right.

'What are you doing?' the man protested, leaping to his feet.

'Sit down,' he commanded. 'I want to take a good look at your face.'

This time the worm was the one to laugh: 'Toad-face,' he taunted, 'a toad through and through.'

The toad did not take this badly, in fact he even posed. 'My profile?' he asked. 'Would you like to see my profile?' He pulled his head back. 'Like this,' he explained, 'you can get a better look at my jaw.'

He studied the face of the toad, taking his time and thinking that perhaps his name did not suit him. At first, more than a toad, he was reminded of a big dog with a pug nose, rheumy eyes and two sprigs of greyish hair flopping over its ears. His neck was non-existent so that his head grew like a pyramid out of his wide shoulders. On the other hand, the character was wearing a greenish jacket, shiny in places, which made him decide that toad was a fairly satisfactory name for him.

'Toad will do,' he conceded. 'Now let's see the worm.'

But the worm got up and retreated into the corner with the washbasin: 'No one is going to inspect me,' he declared.

'Oh, that's a good one!' he exclaimed. 'And why not?'

'Go on, be good,' the toad intervened. 'Show the gentleman your chin. Can't you see how it interests him?'

After some hesitation, the worm raised his head, jutting it forward towards the light without leaving his corner, in fact holding on to the basin with one hand. At this angle, the light picked out a line that descended from his slimy lip to the top of his chest without a break. Rather than receding, his chin was absent, except for a protuberance that could be taken for a simple swelling of the shape of a neck which was basically serpentine. At the top of this neck, the mouth was more or less round and the teeth emerged in a lethal circularity which he assumed was peculiar to maggots.

'Yes!' he concluded. 'Worm! Just the name!'

After these pronouncements, things seemed to calm down. The rain now made only a steady hum and the thunderclaps sounded more distant. The two had gone back to sipping their drinks but were now more ruminative than argumentative.

'So you're always on the door until late at night with your whore?' the toad asked at a certain point.

'No, no,' the worm said calmly. 'We were on our way back from the restaurant when we happened to see you. And anyway she is not my whore. Of course that's her profession, no one denies it, but as far as I am concerned she is only my lodger.'

'Lying little worm,' the toad scolded him mockingly. 'Do you take me for the Vice Squad!'

They both rocked with laughter.

'All right,' the worm finally said, 'I'm not the type who beats women. In other words, it is more from friendship than profit.

'I believe you!' the toad assured him. 'Anyhow, from what I've seen, she seems to be getting on in years.'

'No, no, no! She's as fresh as a rose.'

The toad accepted the worm's protests. Of course, he said, she was undoubtedly an attractive woman ... but after forty, some need to take things a bit more easy. 'And why not?' he concluded. 'It's only right! It's understandable!'

They kept on conversing politely, and through no merit of their own their small talk eventually took on an air of noble detachment. As if to say: these words, despite their immediate verbal sense, are also signs of the inevitable. And in fact the steady hum of rain with its incomprehensible murmuring also alluded to solemn if uncertain prophecies. Dripping and gurgling, something was moving towards its dark conclusion: the force of destiny, it was tempting to say. Certainly all remained comic and ridiculous, because obviously there was nothing noble to be seen here, everything was wretched. It was, he decided, the cellar beneath the tragedy, somewhere below stage where the footsteps of the heroes and voices coming from above could be heard rumbling solemnly, although unintelligibly. Yet, because of these echoes, the place shared in the great dignity of the plot unfolding above their heads, albeit in reverse.

'Are you a cook for the actors?' he asked. And feeling misunderstood, he added, 'Do you ever wash that basin?'

They looked at him politely, without replying.

Appalling, he said to himself. I find it appalling to be with these beasts and yet there is nowhere to go in this gale. So with nothing better to do, he started to listen to the footfalls overhead again. They came and went without warning, these divinities, like ex-machina, and at times they withdrew completely, leaving it to lesser spirits to rustle or murmur like rain at the glass. There was not much structure to all these goings-on, but the gods, of course, also govern chaos and night. When to us everything seems confused and indistinct they are preparing, perhaps with great effort, order and proportion that will later shine forth in the light of day. 'If night comes, day will follow,' the ancients used to say. In any case, he reflected, even night and the hidden must have their own logic. Not the serpentine logic of political or financial machinations but a direct logic as in tragedy; a logic which in this case proclaimed itself for him as though through some profound dignity underlying his own thoughts. But what tragedy did he have in mind? Perhaps Thyestes, perhaps Tamberlaine, according to whether his thoughts inclined more towards the ancients or the moderns.

Of course all this had nothing to do with his being shut up in a room under a skylight in the company of thieves and pimps. And yet, he suspected, in the undeniably turbid depths of the human mind in general there was a sort of Latin grandeur which, albeit denied or in fact derided, functioned as a remedy for the squalor of circumstances. In any case, the roar of thunder in itself had nothing ignoble about it; in fact in its crescendos he seemed to detect a certain baroque tournure that harmonised with some hidden sentiment. And further, straining to hear, apart from a few farts from the wretched people with him, it was possible to discern other faint or very feeble sounds, estimable in their own way all the same: equally attuned to hidden feelings, but this time delicate, even elegant ones.

'Did I doze off?' he abruptly asked the toad, who at that moment, with his behind half off his chair and his rheumy eyes about a foot from his lantern jaw, was peering at him intently.

The shock made the toad jump backwards and almost upset his chair.

'Well, what's there to stare at?' he repeated, turning this time to the worm. And because the two said nothing he went on to explain in considerable detail that sometimes he pretended to doze off so as to tempt certain simpletons to steal his wallet, thinking he was sound asleep, in which case he would take the opportunity to smash one or two faces. Smashing snouts with a couple of good clouts, he declared, was the action that gave him most pleasure, and had brought him renown, glory even.

'How I like it!' he exclaimed. 'Would you fancy a few whacks apiece by any chance, just to see what it's like? Just for a try? Nothing too hard, of course.'

The two politely declined: No, no, there was no need to go to the trouble.

'As you wish' he agreed, and without deeming them worthy of further attention he resumed reasoning with himself about what he had provisionally called the turbid dignity at the bottom of the human mind. It is not, he told himself, that one never manages to discern anything there. There is, yes, a buried text, this is true; but all the same, if only at random, every so often some passages surface in the shape of legible traces. Even if there is no order to them, some passages are legible, if not to the letter, at least their sense. For example, now despite the rain he had suddenly recalled that story about the sun that sets in the east: that is, which halts at midday and turns back along its previous path. A sun in reverse, then. It is from the classics, but where? he pondered.

Certainly, wherever it was, this reverse sun, lugubrious as it was, delighted him. It explains many things, particularly those with a front and back, he said to himself, not to mention that the reverse of the medal is sometimes the transmitter of logic. For instance, once he had seen an unforgettable orchard, all in blossom. Apples and cherries, all flowering at the same time. Of course some flowers fell due to their age even without a breeze, but the overall picture remained intact; flowers everywhere against the sky, the clouds, the mountains. In the midst of all this flowering, however, he suspected (rather he knew about) a reverse side: flat and blank like the back of a postcard. This called to mind the post, the times of the mail trains, the weather as well (that is the light and the hour of day in which the postcard would be delivered to its destination), and suggested an interpretation much more uncertain and even oppressive, utterly different from the orchard in blossom. Now the card had arrived; the recipient, after a glance put it on the side of the table next to her coffee pot and the jam; it was raining outside the window, it would probably rain for days to come, and altogether it could reasonably be predicted that it would rain year after year for the greater part of time, with the sun as rare as a chance glimpse of distant blossoming orchards.

All right, he admitted to himself, aside from this story about the postcard which perhaps didn't make much sense, a reverse side could be hypothesized which would make even the most abstruse appearances legible, at least in the manner of allegories. But unlike those few allegories whose unequivocal meaning has been elucidated in their time, these vague allegories that he hypothesized have such a provisional and shifting sense that it is no help to pay much attention to it. What is important is that even the flimsiest allegories, given the will, by hook or by crook can be made to yield some sense, albeit provisional. What more could one wish? The fact is that at the very moment when life everywhere seems to be stagnating meaninglessly the plot may be advancing along other routes, perhaps even reversing, like a sun setting in the east.

That is how it must be, he concluded, satisfied. 'That's how it is!' he declared, thumping the table, more to shake the two out of their torpor than to affirm anything. 'It's nothing,' he added to reassure them. 'Actually as soon as it's four o'clock, let's all go to the cafe at the station.'

'It is still closed at four,' declared the worm. 'It opens at five.'

'No,' said the toad, 'I've found it open at four-thirty. I often take the train early in the morning.'

'To pick the pockets of dozing passengers,' explained the worm.

The two exchanged sidelong glances, but without animosity, and after a few seconds they both let their heads drop on their chests at the same moment, overwhelmed by sleep.

After all, he thought, it is possible they are pretending to be asleep to trick me. If I followed their example and fell asleep, they could try to do away with me on the sly. He discarded the idea as unlikely. They would need a pistol at least, he thought, and they were not the type for pistols. Yet once invoked the idea of death lingered in his mind. Perhaps, he hazarded, what advances unstoppably, even if in reverse, is really death.

He shrugged off the thought with irritation. No! He didn't like the idea of death; in reality all the conventions to do with the dead annoyed him, too. What sprung to mind was the series of phrases that since earliest childhood he had heard about death. Mors tua vita mea, for example; or the story about going towards the dark, entering the darkness and staying there until the end of time. 'Oh darkness, my homeland,' he found himself saying, and by analogy: 'Oh my America, my new found land!' What a bore! It is certainly true that death is boring.

At this point, had he been in his own bed, he would have turned onto his other side to shake off his discontent, but since he couldn't do that in a seated position, his discontent only grew. Perhaps, he said to himself, between discontent and death there is also an analogy. His dead mother looked discontented. Her habitual peevish scowl had vanished, and lying on her back she appeared to be sleeping a sad and boring sleep in which he imagined thoughts or images, if they still persist, arrive unrelated, without context, without resembling anything and above all without the order of priorities which our desire usually imposes on them. Ideas therefore perhaps continue eternally, but their estranged eternity can only be boring.

'By the way,' he said, thumping the table again. 'Wasn't it full moon tonight?'

The worm stretched: 'Whatever, the moon must have set by

now!'

'So what?' he replied. 'The full moon's influence lasts all night. That's why it's said that lunatics go berserk, whether the skies are rainy or clear.'

'So what do these loonies do?' the toad asked.

'Well,' he said, with a vague gesture. 'They go hunting, I suppose. Nothing alarming,' he added quickly. 'They catch little creatures and tear them to pieces: toads, worms, worthless things like that. You don't happen to think I'm a lunatic?' he asked after a pause.

'We don't believe this nonsense about the moon' the worm said haughtily.

'And yet you do believe the moon has given your whore diarrhoea,' the toad interjected.

'I was talking about another moon,' the worm explained contritely, 'a metaphoric moon.'

This duplication of moons, one apparently real and the other declaredly metaphorical, each pale and still in the midst of the clouds fleeing in the storm, suddenly prompted an idea perhaps more commonplace but more plausible than his many previous ideas about his mother's death. Looking at that face, he saw something passing over it. 'It is the angel of death passing by,' they had told him. But already even then he had seen that a different angel was passing, most likely the other, the angel of life. All life was passing from that face: passing and fleeing, shadow after shadow fleeing and passing, leaving him alone, ever more distant, ever more lost. Oh why, he wondered, why can't we halt between one shadow and the next? Why not rest in a moment of light? And seeing the flight continue implacably, he had flung himself on the floor in despair, beating his fists on the parquet.

They had picked him up and flung him out, scolding him severely for his lack of dignity. 'What a beast!' his uncle had said. 'I can't see how he can ever grow up to be a man!' Never mind. Perhaps the two moons only had some bearing because of this idea of his mother's death; one moon alone, whether real or metaphorical, was enough and it was growing. It was more a moon-word, uttered in the dark or by the light of an electric bulb in a lurid hovel like the one he was in now: a moon that could not manage to elude the clutches of the darkness in which it had been invoked. A moon of remote epochs too, invoked by wandering shepherds on the Asian steppes, no longer shedding any visible light, and yet which spread as far as the eye could see the boredom and the sadness of death.

And looking around, or rather without looking but mentally gazing around the place, he felt he recognized the same sadness in verbal form in the names of things and even in the adjectives with which he kept on trying to qualify them. Everything seemed already in the past to him: the floor of square bricks set in red and white concrete, the wooden table with its white enamel paint, heavily chipped and scratched, the tray, the glasses: all were furnishings for an existence that was over.

Behind him, in the corner beneath the bulb hanging against the wall from a twisted wire, he knew there was a bed on which the worm presumably slept, and beyond this a door which led to the room where the whore was sleeping, and next to her room, the door to the toilet. They had come in by the door near the corner to his left, a double door in the outer wall of the dwelling which was thick enough for both panels of the street door to be left open. The inner door, composed of a single panel with a pane of frosted glass in its upper section was now closed, and against this glass the lightbulb projected his head in profile complete with lantern jaw and the silhouette of his chest in oblique but sharply defined shadow, and more vaguely, other shadows representing the coffeepot, the bottle and the two cups on the table. On another wall beyond the door, the other two characters' shadows, being located along the same barely diverging beam of light overlapped or partially split according to their movements. In the corner behind the table was a washbasin and beyond that the two burner rings, one of which the worm had used earlier to prepare their coffee. On the wall above was a shelf from which after due payment the worm had fetched down two bottles of brandy, the second of which was now an object of dispute between him and the toad. The four walls, originally painted yellow, had been patched with paler plaster in preparation for repainting.

The room, even when described in detail, remained a fragmented and disconnected place, as in certain confused memories in which objects with an obvious relationship, like bread and salami, are often situated a great distance apart, while other pairs, like chamberpots and bottles are right next to each other without even a comma between, as though vaunting a bogus affinity.

Everything looked bogus in a certain way, not only in the prolix description he had made of the place, but in an inexplicable persistence that things had of remaining present and around without there being any need for them, and yet, as the worm had said, almost with a metaphoric function.

'Time to change mode,' he cautioned himself. 'Must try another manner now!'

'What manners would the gentleman prefer?' asked the toad, putting his glass down and wiping his lip, winking at the worm.

The worm also snickered slyly, hiding his mouth with his hand.

'That's right! What manner?' he agreed, lost in thought. 'Perhaps,' he proposed, 'we could do without metaphors. Metaphors endure ...' he explained, 'they transcend the occasions for which they are used and one finds them around without any longer knowing why.'

The two looked at him speechlessly, especially the worm, who opened his mouth to say something at a certain point, but changed his mind and silently closed it again.

'Perhaps he's talking about some whore,' the toad conjectured.

'Ah!' nodded the worm.

The rain died down and at a certain point stopped entirely. Now all that could be heard was the gurgling in the gutters, and even this soon subsided to a murmur, suspended in the silence almost in memory of the past drenching. In the skylight a streak of brightness wavered for an instant: perhaps distant lightning, perhaps a beam of the setting moon threading its way through a hole in the clouds towards the horizon. So then why such desperation now, since all of us at one time or another have to become resigned? In the short term, taking resignation or rather desperation (which is basically the same) in small doses it is always possible that something may improve. Prudent sips of desperation seemed acceptable to him at that moment; they produced a bland burning feeling and a slight tightening of his heart, but as he went on, by slow accumulation, his stomach filled his entire chest cavity with heavy air and shitty vapours.

'Damn' he mumbled and exploded in a most sonorous belch.

'Ha, ha!' the two laughed as one.

'It's that garbage you gave me to drink!' he shouted, banging his fist on the table.

'But if you haven't tasted a drop ...' the worm objected.

He flung his arms wide. 'Then it is the moon,' he explained, 'the shitty moon you keep going on about.'

There followed a long somnolent silence.

'Once,' he said eventually, 'on nights of full moon, people put little bowls of rose petals on the window sills.'

'Petals?' croaked the toad. The worm belched, this time receiving from the toad an instant punch on the forehead that sent him flying off his chair.

The little fellow got to his feet again with studied calm.

'Do that again and I'll knife you,' he said, resuming the same position as before.

'Why not knife him right away?' he asked.

'Maybe I'll use my knife on more than one person,' the worm said, looking him in the eye.

He turned to the toad: 'Let's play a game,' he proposed. 'One of us knocks him off his chair with a whack and the other puts him back with another whack. How about it?'

They were silent for some time. Then the toad said: 'He's just a little shit of a worm. Best forget about him!'

He spread his arms again, disappointed: 'As you wish!' he conceded. And then, once more looking around and seeing everything calm and silent (the two still sat grey and glum, saying nothing) it struck him that he was beginning to get used to the place. I now know this disgusting place by heart, he said to himself, so this is what distresses me. Looking more closely, he felt that every stick of furniture had a lethal density about it: when one gets too acquainted with things they become dense without warning. Let's suppose: one takes a stroll in the town where one was born past houses with benevolent ancestral facades, through the municipal gardens with benches carved with familiar names, looking now at a bush, now a tree, now the corner of a house: especially in springtime with the first leaves, it is pleasant to let one's eyes roam about the world, no matter whether this vagabond look actually sees, or merely remembers having seen. Both in imagination and in experience, this is freedom ... or would be freedom, were it not that suddenly, like the screeching of an alarm, the landscape springs closer, corner by corner, thing by thing. Nearby a crow calls out from the trees on an autumn evening. Or it is bright day and the wind in the park blows all the branches together with a great clatter. Or, still in broad daylight, it is the sky thickening with the heavy blue of storm clouds. But by now what does it matter what it is? Everything has closed in, everything has turned crudely dense. Even a pitcher, could he say? Once, for example, a pitcher stood next to an old-fashioned washbasin in a small room heated by a cast-iron stove, while, beyond the panes of a tiny window, mountains and snow were massing. How many years have passed? Ten? Twenty? But why have so many, so very many years passed if on the point of falling asleep one can remember with unalterable precision the immovable density of an earthenware pitcher?

'What time is it?' he asked.

The toad elegantly hitched his sleeve away from his wristwatch: 'Three-twenty.'

'It seems a bit early for the moon to set!' he observed.

'Who said it's setting?' asked the worm.

'Then it is not setting,' he conceded. 'I was mistaken to think it was setting.'

'Well!' said the worm flattered by the malleability of his guest. 'Since you ask me when it sets, it sets. But not as early as this.'

'Perhaps later,' the toad intervened. 'Who knows?'

'And what happens when the moon sets?' he asked in his turn.

The two shrugged their shoulders.

'So then,' he went on, his voice becoming more and more stern, 'why make so much fuss about whether this moon sets or does not set? Can't you find something less stupid to talk about?'

'Did you hear that?' asked the toad.

The worm shrugged. 'Give me a drink,' he said. 'It's better.' And they started discussing which of them had had more to drink.

'Ugly worm!' said the toad at some point, grabbing the bottle by the neck and pulling it to himself. 'You've been paid for two bottles, one by me and one by this gentleman and now you want to drink from "yours"! What do you mean yours?'

'So sorry,' he interrupted them, 'don't you want me to hit you now?' And because no one bothered to reply, he persisted: 'One of you, perhaps?'

'She went for a pee,' the toad said, to change the subject. And since he gave them both a menacing yet puzzled look, they began explaining to him that behind his back a moment ago the woman had come out of the toilet and returned to her room, and they supposed she had not bothered to flush. 'Drunken women are more disgusting than men,' they said and then went on to speculate on the stench of a drunken woman's piss puddles which, in their opinion, contained a stronger chemical than normal human or dog piss. 'More like a cat,' one of them suggested. The other agreed and then, to keep the subject going, they continued to discuss other foul-smelling urine from wolves and tigers, *aquae stigiae, ex nitro, vitriolo, antimonio, arsenico et similibus extillatae.*

'Stop that,' he said.

They were both quiet and in the silence the rain started to patter on the panes with increasing violence.

'That's hail, I think' he said.

'Listen, now it's hailing!' the toad commented, looking up at the skylight. 'If it comes down, that glass will slice us all into little bits, and no doubt about it.'

'Afraid to die?' sneered the worm.

'And you, worm,' retorted the toad, 'aren't you afraid?'

'Not me,' the worm affirmed with rhetorical swagger. 'I say death is nothing. A person doesn't even feel it.'

'Good for you,' the toad applauded. 'That's what I like about you.' And at the same moment he took a swipe at his neck, which the worm just managed to dodge, skipping off the chair.

'I already told you not to do that any more,' the worm said with dignified calm.

'Absolutely,' he agreed. 'There was also talk of knifing. Where's the knife?'

'Let's get this straight,' exclaimed the worm, becoming ever more declamatory. 'In my house I do what I please. And no one (I mean no one) can tell me what to do with a knife.'

He looked at him with genuine astonishment.

'He's really very good!' he declared, turning to the toad. 'He's not only not afraid to die, he's not even afraid to get hit.'

'That's right!' the toad laughed. 'A little worm of quality.' And the worm, still standing with a hand already eloquently raised for another peroration, could not suppress a smirk of satisfaction at the compliment.

Now that the two were reconciled and the worm had sat down again, this time more prudently out of reach of the toad, they began to talk amongst themselves, exchanging news about a few whores who worked various places in town.

'Is there one with long legs?' he asked. 'Have you heard anything of her?'

At first they looked at him in astonishment; then the toad lit up with sudden understanding. 'She is his flame,' he explained to the worm.

He didn't like this expression and to make it clear he gave the table such a thump that a cup flew off and the bottle was about to topple, but was snatched in mid-air by the toad who passed it to the worm for safekeeping.

'I said flame,' the toad apologised, 'because love burns.'

He accepted this explanation and so three other almost clean glasses and the bottle were ceremoniously put back on the table to toast the reconciliation. After pleasantries, they all fell silent; the conversation about whores, which through his own fault had been interrupted so dramatically, didn't seem possible to take up again. The other two seemed to be waiting for him to propose another topic for discussion, almost to make amends.

'You see, worm,' the toad ventured after a while in a didactic tone, 'he who says woman says woe, in which as a matter of interest the rhyme comes sideways.'

'That's very good,' the worm replied. 'I've never heard of sideways rhymes.'

He didn't like their mannered politeness. The affected calm which drunkards sometimes assume, once they have gone beyond the phase of unrestrained raving, gave their discussion the glassy melancholy of drifting over foggy waters.

'Let's see,' he intervened, to bring them back to reality. And pointing a finger at the toad he asked: 'What's your line of work?'

'I collect!' the toad replied enigmatically. But after repeated requests for explanations he spoke of certain debts the dead had with him.

'What debts? Why dead?'

'Dead men tell no tales,' was the reply. But because the worm wanted to know more, he said he had come to a special arrangement with certain undertakers. 'The truth is that a bit of information can get you a long way,' he said. 'With a little bit of information the rest is easy. Not that you need to know all the life and lore of the dead man; obscene or disgusting complaints such as haemorrhoids came in handy. Anyone talking about them in a loud voice reveals familiarity if not friendship, and everyone wants to change the subject.' Besides, he said, most times it was just a matter of putting on an act like a poor miserable wretch suffering a great injustice, falling to his knees and pleading when they wanted to kick him out. Otherwise he scurried around the house, slipping into every room while proclaiming the virtues and merits of the deceased, snatching up whatever he could get his hands on, underpants, letters, slippers, garters. If they tried to beat him up, which happened fairly often, he suddenly claimed that he had been robbed.

The worm approved enthusiastically, and apparently to please him the toad piled on more and more secondary details: the furniture in some apartment, the size of some widow's buttocks, but despite the descriptive profusion, the scenes recounted lacked colour. A crepuscular atmosphere, or actual night, seemed to envelop the adventures of the toad, the creditor of the dead.

'All right,' he said. 'We understand'.

But the worm kept on asking questions: And how much could you get away with saying a dead man owed? And what if they asked him what he looked like when he was alive? What kind of nose he had, or the shape of his jaw? Did he need to see a photograph first?

'Hey, little worm,' the toad asked, laughing, 'do you want to rob me of my profession?'

The worm protested: 'Of course not!' He didn't need such tricks to live. And then he had never liked being beaten.

'Did you have to go far hunting for these dead creditors?' he intervened. 'Did you see anything interesting on the way?'

'Eh?!' said the toad. 'I stick to the district. These country fellows often come to town and get up to all sorts. They can go whoring or get into card games. This is believable: this their families can understand.'

'Fair enough,' he said. 'But in the end, after fifty or a hundred cases of dead men in debt only a few miles apart, doesn't it ever occur to anyone to suspect something and to beat you up or even get out a knife?'

'They suspect something all right,' the toad replied, 'and they certainly don't pay me. They would never pay what's owed, in any case. It's all about not letting me kick up a fuss at the funeral. That's all. And if they know me, they know I will go as far as the cemetery! I'll even go up to the edge of the grave, I will!'

The worm approved: 'Of course,' he said, 'one must never give in.'

He shook his head. 'Perhaps you're right,' he admitted. 'But I still say: If I were you, every once in a while I would take a little trip: for a change, if not as a precaution. Just think,' he said, 'to see new cemeteries, even cremations, not just burials which are all you get in the country.'

He went on to talk about various funeral customs: there were places where everyone had a good drink together after the burial, and sometimes also a meal. Wasn't it good to see these different ways of celebrating the dead? And then, he said, in addition to any educational value, the trip in itself was often pleasant or at least consoling, especially on certain dark nights of the soul. Travelling is good for a person.

'Yes, that's true,' the worm admitted. 'But a little pleasure trip costs and if a woman, for example, has to earn her living, it's better for her to forget about little pleasures.'

He paid no attention: Had they never taken a train at night? 'It's wonderful!' he declared. He went on to talk about empty waiting rooms, with such dim lighting and so silent that the second hands on the electric clocks seemed to move without a murmur. He also tried to describe the almost graphic visibility of the cold, when the wind tossed rubbish along empty pavements in the dark of night; but, he insisted, what at least for him was so cheering was to see what turned up unannounced; what emerged from the depths of darkness and seemed to come up to him in a friendly way. Above all he liked the vaporous quality of the wind, especially if cold, when it wafted improbable things along and made them look newly washed. Also when travelling at night, looking out of the window, it was impossible to see beyond the streak of light projected by the moving train which cut the countryside into small fragmentary glimpses: a tree, the door of a kitchen, a sloping escarpment full of wild herbs; in other words, quick happy flashes like winks from schoolgirls. 'But what am I saying?' he rubbed his forehead, 'what do you two know about winks from schoolgirls? You only know about piss and shit.'

The toad shrugged. The worm attempted an evasive smirk, but not succeeding, he suddenly turned around on his chair almost in a frenzy.

'Sometimes,' he said, 'we know more than you think.'

'Oh, really?' he asked. 'Let's hear about it.'

'We have also travelled,' said the toad. 'Actually,' he added, turning to the worm, 'we still travel.'

The worm nodded haughtily.

'And then,' the toad continued, 'sometimes one thinks to oneself: tomorrow I'll take the train. I'll go to the country, if nothing else. One could, I mean. Theoretically at least, it is always possible to take the train.'

'I'll grant you that,' he agreed.

'So now you see,' said the toad.

At this point the worm abandoned his angry reserve. He placed a hand on the toad's arm to stop him from talking.

'She,' he said pointing his finger at the bedroom door, 'when she gets in a bad mood she always says she wants to go away. "Tomorrow I'll take the train!" she shouts. And I say sweetly: "Go ahead and take it. But where will you go if you don't have a passport?" Haha!' he laughed, slapping the toad on the back '"If you don't have a passport?" That's a good one, eh?'

The toad considered him thoughtfully. 'And how does she reply?' he asked.

'Bah!' the worm said, making a sweeping gesture with his arm. 'She weeps, but to herself, without making a scene. She knows she has no more time to go away. She's too old for that.'

The toad concurred and they both started to talk about the crazy ideas whores get.

To take his mind off those voices that drunkenness had turned querulous and uncertain, he began to think about a journey together with the whore who was too old to go away. He imagined entering the room to invite her on the journey. 'Come on, get up!' he would say. To be precise, he imagined creeping into her room almost on the sly, perhaps even holding his nose for a moment. He might also open the window, because the night, although it was damp and at times windy, was not very cold: there were a great many stars and over the horizon the translucent reflections of the setting moon streaked the darkness of the sky. Or, since he didn't know precisely when the moon set, he might leave things more vague, keeping the window closed, with the slow dripping from the gutters on the other side of the glass, and just might go up to the window and say: 'It has stopped raining!' Then he would start recapitulating what the men had said about her in the course of the night, not a true summary, just random confidences, slipping in what he thought might please her. In other words, his tone was casual, even distracted, and he often left pauses between one report and the next, long enough for something of the slow passage of night-time to reach them inside the room.

Meanwhile through the window he would watch the dimming of the sparkling stars. The sky showed more paleness than light, as the tenuous luminosity of the day was taking hold. Now the day had all but begun, and yet the night persisted. Day came with great reluctance. The change of light looked so laboured that rather than coming to an end night seemed to proceed beyond its firm boundaries, pushing the time of shadows ever further on. Even the clouds which he imagined in perfect stillness gathered along the rim of the horizon declared that reality did not intend to change register for the moment. There was time. Perhaps for the moment, or at least this instant, both of them, he and the drunken woman still had time.

'What time is it?' he asked.

It was a quarter past four Saturday November 28th, the toad reported after consulting his watch. He nodded, thinking that now there was nothing querulous and uncertain in the declarations about the hour and the day.

'Well, then,' he said, 'when shall we go out?'

The worm looked evasive and the toad started to speak once more about his dead people.

'What was this story about the country?' he asked, to change the subject.

The toad had never spoken of the country, but since the conversation turned to country matters he started talking about a widow and her house. The widow was attractive and her house was rather run-down but not ugly. It was set in about an acre of land, about three miles from the nearest town. Then he added that it had four fairly large rooms on the ground floor and six smaller ones on the floor above; wood was stored in the attic. There was water and light, but no latrine. There was an old dungpit in corrugated sheet iron about ten yards away and a tap in the kitchen. As he spoke his tone remained earnest and yet hesitant as though tackling a difficult subject. 'The trouble is,' he said finally, 'I can't convince her. That is, since she is a widow and all this is hers, the solution would be for me to marry her; but once when I almost managed to get on top of her by slapping her around, just as I let go of her a moment to unbutton she wriggles free and runs for her shotgun. I didn't think it was loaded, and got a volley right in the belly.'

'Boom!' the worm said. 'You'd be dead ...'

'Dirty sea salt,' the toad explained, 'She keeps her gun loaded with sea salt to shoot at the pants of kids who come to steal her fruit. So thanks to that bit of lard that pads any respectable stomach, I had to spend a day and a night soaking in a hot bath to leech out the salt.'

'So you also took a bath,' the worm commented. 'Life is full of surprises!'

The toad nodded thoughtfully: 'I would have liked the house,' he said, with a look of regret on his face.

The worm snickered, more or less to himself. Now probably also because the rain had stopped, the silence in the room weighed more heavily than before. He also was quiet, thinking about the silence. He felt that every time silence intervened something that first had seemed negligible or even as ridiculous as the widow's house described by the toad acquired an appearance of order and good design, an elegant severity. Now that the house was wrapped in silence and hopefully moonlight, despite the abandon and neglect in which it had been left to decay, as the toad said, it aroused a sort of affectionate fellow feeling in him. He imagined the house creaking in the rigid solitude of a harsh winter, or enclosed in itself, doors and windows shuttered against the monotonous blaze of the summer sun ... What sort of life was possible in that house? Putting himself in the place of the toad out of love for the house, he saw himself frugal, knowledgeable, patient, while he wandered around the garden by the light of the moon. The acre of land that had been mentioned was full of wild apple trees which now in winter entwined their bare branches together to trap the white of the moon in nets of various sizes.

'What can be done with these trees?' the lady of the house wondered. 'In any case,' she added, 'I'll see they are pruned.'

They walked together along the gravel path towards the house. Above the door but to one side, on the left next to the lintel, a small caged lamp cast a faint light, and radiated geometrical shadows against the facade, but the far ends were lost in the dark. They reached the door and went in, and a little later, sitting in front of a lighted fire, she explained that the prunings from the tree would make good firewood in a year.

This kind of conversation, or perhaps the firelight flaring from time to time, let the seriousness of winter engulf them. Without saying so, without desiring it and perhaps without even thinking it might be possible, they thought of growing old together in that house or, as the saying goes, of living together to the end of their days. He felt these final days coming slowly, becoming more densely foggy with every winter, until one could detect the ultimate winter from the thickness of the fog.

'Miserable worm, you are going to die!' the toad declared, morosely gazing at the now empty bottle. 'Disgusting vile worm,' he chanted over and over again. 'You are worse than a pig, worse than a chicken,' he said, shaking his head pityingly.

The worm looked at him laughing and giving it back to him: 'Worm! Worm! Cluck – cluck! What's the sense of constantly repeating it? I also judge myself,' he said finally. 'What do you think?' And since the others were looking at him with astonishment, he went on: 'Yes, gentlemen: I see myself and use the word "he" meaning the author of my actions and also of my thoughts. And conversely, if I insist on saying "I" for my deeds and my days, then it is "he" who judges me. But after all, I ask myself, who is truly the author of what I say? I or the other? So who thinks and eats and drinks and talks and fucks?'

'And yet one thing is sure,' the toad scoffed. 'You are the one who always gets drunk, and not the other.'

'What difference is there?' the worm asked. 'And between you and me,' he insisted, 'where's the difference?' He raised a finger contentiously. 'Don't you understand that extending the doubt about this I-he, every difference between men, if there is any, also looks weak, very weak. Even between Rothschild and ...'

'So now you are a Rothschild?' the toad asked sternly.

'No,' the worm responded, punctuating his words with his upraised finger. 'This weakness in the difference signifies only that no one is completely himself, except in appearance, and that all are, at least parenthetically and marginally, possibly another. Perhaps the same other for everyone: that other who bears the burdens of everyone: of worms, of toads, of sons of whores, too. Drunk or sober, everyone merry and bright. What's so shocking? Why limit grace?'

The toad let out a roar: 'But look what we have to listen to from a vile drunken worm. No, worm!' he shouted. 'You are the vomit, the urinal, the dungheap of the world. There is nothing else. No grace, no hope for you. Look in the mirror! If you looked at yourself a bit more, you would understand that no one can be in your place but you.'

He watched them with curiosity and surprise.

'Did you hear?' the toad asked, gasping and wiping away the saliva with the back of his hand. 'What do you think? Tell him!'

He shook his head, laughing: 'You are both right,' he decreed. 'Besides, drunks always end up all being right together and I am right with you.'

His verdict, enunciated with the clarity of an official document, seemed to please one more and the other less, but both accepted it without explicit reservations, thus putting an end to the nocturnal confusion. Clarity is a very beautiful thing, he thought. With the daylight beginning to show through the skylight a certain blustering defiance seemed to be in reserve or implicit in the brightness of the window, as in a space too open, salty and windy.

The worm in the meantime was snickering to himself, creasing his cheeks and his temples under his soft sticky hair which on the right, that is on the side of the light, looked more pale. The faint sound of the snicker, a sort of intermittent chirrup, was the only noise in the room for some time, until, through the door left ajar, the now calm snoring of the whore in the other room reached their ears.

In the brief interval of solitude, that chirruping seemed to have favoured the transformation of his thoughts. Gone irretrievably were the paragraphs about journeys, the house in the country, and even death and the other places of the imagination that he had contrived with questionable success to frequent in the course of the night; now he found himself facing a range of ideas like coffee, jam, wind, brioches, which taken one by one were clear and familiar, but now, together, presented themselves like a grey and unexplored city.

# On translating *Sleep*

Ann Colcord

The central character of this enthralling novel by Michele Spina is preoccupied with his sleeping difficulties, and traces a dream-like path around a town searching for the missed, the incomplete, the unfulfilled, the misunderstood, the bungled opportunity so that he can try again, and achieve a sound sleep. Or is sleep more a matter of acquiring than achieving? The narrative ripples, drawing mingling levels of depth to the surface, with a weird sense of fantasy.

Emma Spina introduced me to the Italian text some years ago, which her husband completed just before his death in 1990. I found it both haunting and daunting, then, as I have continued to do. She encouraged me to translate the work, and helped unstintingly. Brian Horne offered suggestions in moral theology when I was trying to convey in English the first words of the text about the interior courtyard, the inner forum, without losing the spirit of the Italian. The late Rob Baker offered great encouragement. At a later stage Helen Holder made a great many helpful suggestions. So did Giuliana Giglio and Edoardo Berlendis.

Then at an even later stage Hugh Shankland enthralled me with his fervour to hone the translation further. The result was greater accuracy and clarity. His thoroughness and insights, his imagination and his stamina reminded me of a sculptor's. He came to grips with the text, trying to release the subtle and precise substance of the novel from obdurate blocks of English. Sometimes it seemed more like trying to craft a goblet or locate a glass or a drinking vessel of some sort appropriate for the content of a word or a phrase.

Defining the boundaries of decorum in translation was a problem I was glad to be able to share. How to deal with all the beating up, trouncing, hitting, boxing on the ears, cuffing, slapping, whacking, wallops and the repeated use of the word 'culo' in Italian. Should it be translated 'ass' or 'arse' – or bottom, or backside, or what? How does the voltage in Italian fit with an English word, or is more than one needed? In principle, I tried to hold to a single word whenever an Italian word was frequently used, so it would resonate, reverberate, pivot the narrative and pin it down.

Compiutezza was translated not finished, or completed, but fulfilled. Not well being but fulfilment. And salute in Italian is a word for both health and salvation in The Divine Comedy. Thanks to his interventions, thorough, imaginative, scrupulous, finicky ones, and his corrections and his beguiling acting out of the dialogue (occasionally) the novel took on sharper focus. And thanks to the publisher for allowing the deadline for the final translation to be pushed back to accommodate the harrowing delays while Shankland perfected the changes which he suggested to me.

And other problems we could discuss included the verb the protagonist's mother used about his friends: dropped you? Discarded you? Left you out? The harshness of his mother seemed best rendered through repetition: They've dropped you, haven't they?

Indulgent, considerate, kind represented an opposite value in this text to grim, severe, stern. And is the setting a city or a town? (the setting is a town, the references are to cities).

The rag, trash, garbage flying around was a way to indicate sympathy for underdogs. In the 30's the Fascists tended to round up the small fry, which happened later with Mafia arrests, but the important schemers throughout Italian history in the past century have usually been safe, and only the minor culprits caught.

A translator not only works with the words of the text and the sense they make, but is concerned with rhythms and pulse. It seems like dancing, almost waltzing with the text, to keep pace with it. This is the part that is particularly hard to share. Collaboration occasionally feels like 'cutting in' and stumbles, and stiffening because rhythm is too intangible to be defended.

He questioned the appropriate words for the threshold of sleep. At one time he would prefer to call it the border, and we discussed the boundary, the rim, all those margins, the edge of the horizon where the clouds cluster, the entrance to the brothel, the view from the door, the rules of the threshold, the laws of the brink, the rules that govern the brink of sleep: this was the chapter title, this was the wording we settled on. The word fruscio recurs, and at times the translation used the word rustle, at others, rumble, or hum: in the last pages of part 1 his secretary departs with a rustle. Leaves rustle, rain makes a rustling sound, and the various noises of a storm were important to the novel. The description of light and shade, the sheen, or shine or gleam of the sky, or the front door, concealed (or did it?) the presence of mystery, or enlightenment, or the threat of malice or bad luck. Meaning was to be found under the surface, behind the veil. Logic and processes of thought were likened to threads, and a ball, and a skein of the unthinkable.

And what about the sun going into reverse? The sun backing up? The sun sliding backwards? The sun setting in the East? It has been fascinating to give provisional answers to many questions. *Sleep* is a novel full of allusions, dense with insight and wisdom, alluring with its hidden depths and shifting irony and its mirrors into our memory. Unbounded thanks to Emma Spina and Hugh Shankland for all they have done to help with the English translation.